PRAISE FOR *LIZZIE!*

"SMART, SPUNKY, AND DELIGHTFULLY QUIRKY, LIZZIE IS AN
UNFORGETTABLE HEROINE."
— KYOKO MORI, AUTHOR OF *SHIZUKO'S DAUGHTER*

"THIS IS THE CAPTIVATING YOUNG ADULT NOVEL WE MIGHT WELL
EXPECT FROM MAXINE KUMIN, WHOSE POEMS ARE SOME OF AMERICA'S
BEST CRAFTED AND MOST ENJOYABLE."
— X. J. KENNEDY, POET AND AUTHOR OF *THE OWLSTONE CROWN*

"I LOVE *LIZZIE!* — THE NOVEL AND THE DELIGHTFUL,
SPIRITED GIRL AT THE HEART OF IT."
— HILMA WOLITZER, AUTHOR OF *INTRODUCING SHIRLEY BRAVERMAN* AND *OUT OF LOVE*

"AS A BLIND AUTHOR AND LOVER OF LITERATURE, I HAVE ALWAYS
WANTED TO READ A STORY ABOUT A HERO OR HEROINE WITH A
DISABILITY WHOSE DISABILITY ISN'T CENTRAL TO THE PLOT. *LIZZIE!*
IS A WONDERFUL READ ABOUT JUST SUCH A CHARACTER."
— LAURIE RUBIN, AUTHOR OF *DO YOU DREAM IN COLOR?*

LIZZIE!

LIZZIE!

MAXINE KUMIN

ILLUSTRATIONS BY ELLIOTT GILBERT

SEVEN STORIES PRESS
TRIANGLE SQUARE books for young readers
NEW YORK • OAKLAND

Seven Stories Press
140 Watts Street
New York, NY 10013
www.sevenstories.com

College professors may order free examination copies of Seven Stories Press titles. To order, visit www.sevenstories.com/textbook or send a fax on school letterhead to (212) 226-1411

Kumin, Maxine, 1925-2014
 Lizzie! / by Maxine Kumin.
    pages cm
 Summary: A bright, curious girl in a wheelchair who enjoys visiting a petting zoo in her Florida town uncovers a mystery surrounding a shack full of screeching monkeys.
  ISBN 978-1-60980-518-0 (hardback)
 [1. Wheelchairs--Fiction. 2. Paralysis--Fiction. 3. People with disabilities--Fiction. 4. Animals--Treatment--Fiction. 5. Mystery and detective stories.] I. Title.
  PZ7.K949017Li 2014
  [E]--dc23
                    2013025662

Printed in the United States of America

9 8 7 6 5 4 3 2 1

Again, for Judith

FOREWORD

If you think this is just some sweet sappy story about two kids in wheelchairs and a dear patient single mother, get over it. You could live your whole life and not have this much stuff happen. This is my AUTOBIOGRAPHY! It took me almost a whole year to write it and I promise you it is not boring. So either start reading or shut this book now. It's up to you.

Lizzie

CHAPTER 1

*L*izzie stop! Stop Lizzie!*" Those were the last words
I heard before I did a cannonball off the diving
board and slipped and split the back of my head
open on the edge of the pool. I bled so much that the whole
deep end turned pink. At least that's what my best friend
Trippy—short for Triple A—told me a week later when she
came to see me in the hospital. Her real name is Ashley
Anne Addington and she likes her nickname which by the
way I thought up.

"I swear it Lizzie. Pink as a petunia. Here."

Trippy is a major liar. She says she just exaggerates. If my
whole body bled dry it wouldn't turn the pool pink. The
human body only contains ten pints of blood. And by the
way I don't like commas. They're too curly all over the page
so you'll see I don't use them very often.

She brought me a whole box of peanut brittle my favorite
food. I wasn't supposed to eat it because it gets stuck in my
braces. But nothing like that mattered anymore. If I wanted
ice cream for breakfast I could have it. That's what made me
cry but I never let anybody see me except a couple of times
my mom. We both knew everything changed with that one
cannonball off the bare board. They'd taken the old coconut

matting off to replace it but they hadn't put up a sign saying KEEP OFF.

I don't remember the ambulance ride or anything much about the whole rest of the day. When I came to I was in the hospital in the I See You which stands for Intensive Care Unit and my legs didn't work at all. I couldn't even feel them.

That was two years ago. I miss the whole gang of us faculty brats who used to horse around the indoor pool. Most of all I missed Trippy but guess what? She just flew down to Florida to visit us. We live in a neat little cottage Mom bought this year once the lawsuit got settled. Trippy's going to stay ten whole days over her winter break. Flying down here by herself the day after Christmas was her big present. For my big present I got this desk with extra-wide knee-holes I can roll my chair right into. That was all I needed to start writing my autobiography. Trippy read what I've written so far.

"You've got to put commas in, Lizzie. It's too hard for the common everyday goon to read."

Goons is what Trippy always called our gang of girls. In a friendly way, though. As in, "Come on, all you goons, let's go!" But I agreed, so from here on you'll see a few more curlies here and there.

Lots of kids in northern Wisconsin are good swimmers. The winters are so long and cold that the indoor pool is a major playground. Our whole gang of girls could swim in deep water by the time we were four. My mom, a professor of psychology, did laps three times a week. Our favorite thing in the world was doing cannonballs. We always raced to be first off. To jump the highest. To jump the farthest.

Trippy said I need to explain why we live here in Florida now. It's so that I will always be warm. People with spinal cord injuries usually have trouble regulating their body temps, and you can count me in on that. While I was still in the hospital I went downstairs to the rehab clinic every day. The PTs—that stands for physical therapists—were like my older sisters. Like my older sisters would have been if I hadn't been an only child. My mom is what they call a single mother. My father was a sperm from a sperm bank in California that specializes in sperm from very intelligent men. And that's probably why I'm in the eighth grade, even though I'm only eleven and a half.

Anyway, the PTs were my cheerleaders egging me on. Every morning they got me out of bed and fitted me with braces. In the big treatment room I met kids who'd been in car crashes and fallen from ladders and off runaway horses. There we all were, trying to learn how to walk again. Or tie our shoes. Or fit the simplest pieces into a puzzle.

So what I figured out was it could have been a whole lot worse. My spinal cord wasn't cut in two—*severed* is the word doctors use. It was "shocked," but nobody could say if I would ever get any feeling back in my dead legs.

Even though she had plenty of other things to do, Trippy came to watch lots of afternoons. "Don't mind me, I'm just here to kibitz," she'd say, and they'd let her hang around.

The PTs worked my arms and legs. They strapped me to machines with timers that beeped when I'd done enough arm pulls and leg presses, but I can't really feel what my legs are doing, so I just pushed as hard as I could. Trippy was there, kneeling down by the leg machine. "Come on, you old goon you, you can do two more," she'd yell. She'd make me so mad that I did.

The PTs gave me rewards of balloons and sticks of gum as if I were a three-year-old. When I took my first step hanging onto the parallel bars without one of them holding me up by the belt tied around my waist, they whistled and cheered. I was holding on for dear life.

"Look at you, you old goon you! Hip hip! Three cheers!" Trippy yelled.

I was glad Trippy was there to see. That was a good day. I'm supposed to get upright every day and use my quad canes to take five steps. But I still need the wheelchair to go beyond the front door or back porch.

CHAPTER 2

The day after Trippy got here we went to Wilderwood to see the bear cubs. Mom and I go about once a week to HENRY'Z PETTING ZOO. That's what his sign says, he thinks the *Z* is cute. His name is Henry Eberly but Henry the Huge is what Mom and I call him behind his back. He is so fat he has to hold his pants up with two belts fastened together.

Henry tells people that the cubs' mother was shot by a hunter and that's how come he got to raise them by himself. Well, that's a lie. Orphaned cubs have to be turned over to the Florida Fish and Wildlife Conservation Commission and they'd never send them to some little roadside zoo. You can find that out online in two secs. You can also go to their website *myfwc.com* in case you want to find out more about what they do and it's not just black bears. For instance, the manatee death toll this year is double the usual number and they tell you why.

"Five dollars a week to get to play with baby bears? Wow! How neat is that?" Trippy said. "It's worth five hundred dollars! How far away is it?"

"It's all back roads," my mom said. "A little more than half an hour."

But I knew exactly. "It's seventeen-point-eight miles. Their names are Buddy and Blossom. I used to be able to snuggle them both in my wheelchair with me but now they're getting too big."

"But golly, goonie, imagine getting to cuddle real live bears! That's way beyond sweet!"

Trippy made me feel lucky. But I told her it wasn't so terrific anymore. "The thing is, they're getting scratchy, they start fighting to get down and Buddy nipped my ear the last time. It only bled a little. Henry says he's going to have to let them go pretty soon. Then his cat had kittens and I got to keep one of them, Tigger. She's a calico and calicos are always female. Well, almost always, we looked it up on Google."

"Tigger out of Winnie-the-Pooh? I wish I had a kitty. Or a dog, I'd take really good care of a dog. But we can't have any pets. My mother is allergic to practically everything in the universe. Including lima beans and perfume."

"I carried Tigger around everywhere at first. Now that she's big enough, she jumps up to my shoulder and we ride around together. I have to close her in the house when it's time to go to school, though." I'm not exactly crazy about school either—except for Josh, but more about that later.

Before we got there, I explained a little about Henry. "He can make anything grow. He can take up a handful of dirt and sniff it—almost eat it—and decide what could grow there."

Trippy made her famous gagging sound at that.

I ignored the sound effects and explained that he's got a humongous vegetable garden with cucumbers climbing up one side of the trellis and beans climbing up the other side.

"Beans all over. Skinny green kinds and flat yellow kinds. Tomatoes everywhere, some of them tied up to stakes and some of them sprawling. Lots of different squashes, kinds I've never heard of and neither has Mom because they probably don't do well up north. Henry says they're Mexican. And eggplant."

"Eggplant, yuck." Trippy rolled her eyes. "I could live my whole life without a single bite of squash, too. But growing your own cukes and tomatoes would be kind of neat."

The best thing about Henry is hearing him talk. I said that at first he was hard to understand.

"I don't know what kind of accent he has but you get used to it after a while. He was telling us about his life, saying his da had been a truck farmer. He grew good carrots and long-day onions and the sweetest *strub-bries*—I love the way he said that word—in the whole state."

"Strub-bries?"

"Yeah, that's how he says strawberries." I went on imitating the way Henry talked about his father.

"'Lotsa things they said wun't grow in Florida, like punkins that need it cool and pineapples that need it hot, he grew 'em good. Jess cuddn't make much of a livin' doin' it.' So Henry says that's how he got into commercial flowers with his ma after his pa died. Snapdragons mostly, because they didn't need the steady heat roses do. 'But hail, they was bringin' flors in from Chile cheaper 'an we could raise 'em, so I quit.'"

I can't do it exactly but *flors* is another great word.

And then we were there. No sign of Henry, but we knew he'd see our car and he'd come out of the house soon.

I showed Trippy his tame iguana. "It's six feet long if you count its tail. Mostly it just lies on a branch of this live oak tree."

"What's this? It looks like a humongous turtle!"

"It's a tortoise that's more than a hundred years old but you hardly ever see it move. Once though, it came out of its shell and took a piece of lettuce from me and I got to see how its wrinkly neck connects to the top and the underneath parts of him and how its eyes are red."

"Red eyes," Trippy said. "How weird is that?"

"I thought maybe they were red with sorrow. Mom said she suspects all old tortoises have red eyes and that this one probably wasn't sad at all. And look over here. Henry's got these two gray African geese with funny red feet and they hiss all day as they waddle around."

There were lots of chickens pecking about in the grass for insects. "They're so tame that if you hold out anything for them to eat you can just pick them up, see?" I leaned out of my chair, scooped up a fat hen, and fed it a raisin I had in my pocket. "Want to try?"

Trippy shook her head. Instead she wandered off to check out the two pygmy goats. "These are pretty cool, Liz. And what about this little donkey? I'd give anything to have a little donkey for a pet."

"He's a burro from out west and he's crazy for carrots. He likes apples, too. Here, hold a piece out flat on your palm like this." I showed her.

Trippy laid the apple slice out on her hand and he scarfed it right up. Then he nuzzled her for another. "Oh I love the way his nose tickles me. It's sweet the way all these guys roam around loose."

I agreed. "There aren't any fences at Wilderwood except over here where he keeps Buddy and Blossom. See that old wrecked truck? That's where they like to sleep. And that piece of sewer pipe? They love to crawl through it and climb on what's left of that big gumbo-limbo tree, so it's not too bad. We always come with pecans, that way they're always glad to see us. Bears love nuts. And Mom always packs apple slices. Carrot chunks too sometimes."

"Gumbo-limbo—what a snazzy name for a tree!"

"Yeah, see, it puts up all these side branches, kind of like a hammock."

"So all this belongs to Henry. I guess he's pretty smart."

"In some ways. But about other things, he isn't—well, he isn't quite bright. I think he knows it too but it doesn't bother him one bit. Like when I ask him to name the last five presidents. Or what is the capital of Indiana? The square root of fifty? He just scratches his head and crosses his eyes."

"Well, come on, Lizzie! Those are way too hard. I don't know all the answers."

I had to grin at that. To tell the truth, neither did I.

And then Henry came out and we had introductions all around. He unlocked the gate to the cubs' enclosure and insisted on wheeling me in. I was perfectly able to wheel myself in but I think he was trying to show off in front of Trippy. Buddy came right over to me. I was able to pull him up on my lap and feed him pecans one by one. I gave Trippy a handful to feed to Blossom, who cuddled with her on a tree limb.

"Nobody would believe this back in the whole entire state of Wisconsin!" she said.

After the bears had cleaned up all the treats, we went off to look at Henry's veggie garden. It's an amazing place. He has a buyer who comes every week to pick up his produce and take it to fancy grocery stores and restaurants in Miami and Fort Lauderdale.

Trippy admired the tomatoes. Some were as big as softballs, others were shaped like tiny pears. "How does he keep it so neat? He must spend hours and hours out here pulling weeds."

I couldn't picture big fat Henry on his knees weeding but Trippy was right. There was hardly a single weed growing up through the mulch. Weeks ago, Henry told me his gardening secret was chicken manure—"It'd make nail parings grow,"—and mulch, which was spoiled hay he raked up from the goats and the burro.

"Once they tromp on it even the least little bit they won't eat it no more but it don't go to waste. I just tuck it around my plants. But I wish I could get some sallet greens, you know, the kinds a leafs folks eat raw from a sallet bowl, they just don't do good here in the heat. They put up one row of leafs and then they bolt. 'Specially spinach; folks like to eat baby spinach leafs."

I asked him what *bolt* means and he told me. "That's when they put up a flower stalk and then it goes to bursten and makes seeds."

When I told Trippy about it, she sympathized. "I'm not crazy about salad but we eat it every night. Mom gets these bunches of red lettuce. I bet Henry'd love to grow them. Does he live all alone here?"

"No, he lives with his mother. I've never seen her, though.

Mom asked him, Is she bedridden? He said no, she gets around as much as she wants. Not much, though. He said he cooks for her but he has to keep it soft now because she can't chew well anymore. He didn't say *well* of course. He said *good*. And when Mom made a sympathetic noise in her throat, he said he's been trying to get her into one of those *a'sister livin'* places. And then he told Mom that as long as she owns this land they say she's too rich to get in.

"And when Mom said, 'You mean you'd have to sell it?' he told her no, because then she'd still be too rich with the house and all. Then I heard him say, 'Might be I could give it away, though.'

"I could tell from the look on Mom's face that she was horrified. She told him not to do anything without a lawyer and she made him promise her. She made him promise not to give away any of his land. Because it might be worth a lot of money—it might be *very valuable*.

"Then he said, 'Well, I wouldn't jess give it away like that. Happens there's a big businessman—you met him, Jeb Blanco? Happens he has his own plane and he flies it in on that ole cow pasture where the dozer smoothed him out a place to land? Him and me, we might make a deal where he owns the land for a good cause but I still live on it, and he gets my momma into a really good *a'sister livin'* place. And then I can travel around. I'd get me one a them movin' homes. I allus wanted to travel around.'"

I filled Trippy in on Jeb Blanco. I described the first time we saw him land. Two men in a big black Lincoln Navigator car came roaring up past Henry's zoo sign and drove straight out to the plane. Then they drove back to Henry's house and

Jeb Blanco got out to talk to Henry. By then the two men were in the backseat and I couldn't really see them because the windows were tinted. Blanco was wearing a bright blue polo shirt with a monogram and the kind of loafers that have tassels on them. Not your average drop-in at a petting zoo, oh, no. He looked like he owned the whole state of Florida. And there was something very familiar about him. I told Trippy I had a feeling I'd seen him before, but where? So I sort of blurted, "Didn't we meet somewhere once? You look . . . like somebody I think I know from somewhere." It was a jerky thing to say. I was embarrassed.

I remember that he laughed and said, "Everybody tells me that, *pequeñita*. I just have the kind of face people are used to looking at." And when I asked him, "Are you here for Buddy and Blossom? Are you here to take them away?" he said, "No, I promise you. I just came to see Henry and his mother."

Because it was the first time we'd met, he extended his hand to my mom. "Jesús Ernesto Blanco," he said. "But call me Jeb. It's from my initials, see? J E B."

And so she had no choice. "Rebecca Peterlinz," Mom said, and shook the hand he reached out to her. It was tanned with a thick gold ring on the little finger and his face matched his hand. We don't sit out in the sun without putting on tons of sun cream but people still do. I have to say that he had a sweet sort of face with deep blue eyes and the kind of rimless glasses you expect to see on a professor. I know this because I saw a ton of professors back in Wisconsin before my accident.

He didn't exactly ask me what happened. People don't

because it's rude. But he sort of took my mom off to one side and I knew he wanted to know had I been born this way. And here I am all this time with a mashed spinal cord. Can't take a step without my quad canes—not even able to swim, really swim, anymore because I have to drag my legs behind me.

CHAPTER 3

Trippy loved our cottage. She loved sleeping on the air mattress Mom had made up for her in my room. She made us promise not to talk all night but of course we did. Half the night, anyway. Trippy raved over our living so close to the water; it was the first time she'd ever seen the ocean. She loved listening to the soft slurp of the waves. She said living on the inlet where you can watch ocean liners leave and come back is better than boss. Living on the inlet is okay. Mom takes me down to the beach just about every afternoon when it's warm enough. She pushes my chair as far as it will go in the sand and then I get out and kind of crawl into the water. I tried not to make a big deal out of it when I scooched out of the wheelchair onto the sand in front of Trippy. Once I'm all the way in I look just about like everybody else, and we had a great time horsing around in the ocean.

"This is way sweet, goonie! The salt water holds you up a lot better than the water in the college pool." After our fingers had turned into prunes, we coasted into shore on the best wave we could find—the waves are really only ripples here at the inlet compared to the real waves farther down the coast.

That was how we dragged out our afternoons on the beach. We dragged them out because we didn't know when we'd get to be together again after this visit. "But now that Grammy and Gramps have moved down here, maybe I'll be coming to Florida a lot," Trippy said.

And I said, "Maybe." We hooked our little fingers together the way we used to when we were just kids.

"What goes up the chimney?" Trippy said.

"Smoke."

"May your wish and my wish never be broke."

"—en," I said and we laughed and sort of hugged.

I miss the girls who were my friends before the accident. I can't say I miss the way they were after, when I couldn't hang out with them on the soccer field after school or go to the movies in a gang Saturday nights. I couldn't talk anymore about the boys who were always acting like idiots in class to impress us. Or at least that's what we thought they were doing. Trippy was the only one who stayed in touch with me. We talked on the phone sometimes and we emailed a lot, but it's hard to stay best friends from a distance. Mom wouldn't let me go on Facebook, which she called a social scourge—look that one up. I have to wait till I turn fourteen. She didn't approve of Skype either. Some of my old more-or-less friends sent Christmas cards and a lot of them were from the kinds of families who always put a Christmas letter in with the card. I hate those letters. They're always about how the whole family went skiing in Colorado and ice fishing on Lake Michigan and what the kids did that summer, hiking and rock climbing.

Meeting people is easy here in Florida. For one thing,

people are outside more. Everybody comes down to the beach, just to walk up and down looking for shells or to exercise their dogs. A lot sit around and play cards or talk about how great it is not to be stuck in the snow and ice. And there I am, either sitting in my wheelchair or crawling back to it. No one could ignore that and even though it's not polite to ask what happened to you, it's also rude not to smile, say hello, and start a conversation.

I guess you could say Teresa and Digger are our best friends here. We met just chatting the way people do on the beach. They never said anything about my wheelchair, which I was just climbing back into that day when Teresa stooped down right next to me to pick up a crushed soda can somebody had left behind and Mom tsk-tsked about people who litter and one thing led to another. After they had introduced themselves, I got introduced too. That was only our first *rendezvous*, which is French and means you present yourself. Pretty soon it got to be a daily beach get-together. It turned out that Digger used to be the police chief of Montandino, a town in California, but then he had a heart attack and they retired to Florida because they have a grown-up daughter who lives here. He says it was only a little heart attack, but Teresa says he lost some of his heart muscle and he needs to take care of what he's still got. She is always after him to take daily walks—he does walk down to the jetty every morning early—and not to eat those dough-nuts that he buys at the 7-Eleven. She wants him to eat fish three times a week for the omega oil. I don't know why it is good for your heart, but Digger said he doesn't like fish, period.

Then I got to introduce Trippy to Teresa and Digger, whose real name is Diego. Their last name is Martinez, and now Teresa's teaching me Spanish. Like *la pequeñita* means little one.

After I explained that Trippy was visiting me from Wisconsin, I said, "Teresa told me she once was a union organizer in California."

Trippy didn't know what that meant. I hadn't known either, until Teresa and I got to talking about a zillion things. And one day she told me about her killer jobs with the migrant fruit pickers and workers in the tomato fields and so on.

I asked Teresa to explain about getting the workers together to ask for things like enough Porta Potties in the lettuce fields. Or higher pay for picking grapes seven days a week when they all got ripe at once.

"Oh, like marching in a line with signs," Trippy said. "Picketing. I've seen that on TV."

"Well, we didn't have picket lines exactly, but we held up signs and shouted slogans till the crops started to rot."

"And then the managers were willing to let you have a union," I added.

Teresa smiled. "Something like that. They were willing to talk about the workers' *grievances*."

That was a new word but I knew right away what it meant. I had a few grievances of my own at Graver Academy from being in a wheelchair and being called crip behind my back. And I hate it when the soccer team huddles before a game and comes up yelling *Be braver be braver forever for Graver.* They don't know Day One about braver. First the horrible headaches after the accident that went on for days, then finding out that I didn't have any feeling in my legs and feeling so sorry for myself that I just wanted to lie in bed and not answer when people came in. I'd pretend to be sleeping. My mom wouldn't let me give up. She kept bringing me the daily puzzles from the morning paper and a new Jane Goodall book I hadn't read yet and so on.

I explained about Trippy's nickname. Digger thought it was pretty neat. He said he got his name when he was a little kid. "I had a shovel and I was always digging."

"For what?"

"For water. Or maybe for gold." We all laughed.

Well, the next day Trippy had to go visit her grandparents, who were snowbirds, people who come to spend the winter in Florida after they retire. They lived about an hour away. Her grandfather drove up to get her and she was going to stay with them one night. We'd still have almost a whole week left to hang out.

"It'll give you more time to work on your autobiography," Trippy said. "So do some more and I'll read it when I get back."

I didn't waste any time.

CHAPTER 4

While Trippy is visiting her grandparents, I am going to write down what my life was like before my accident. I had a best friend Tony next door, who was a year older than I was. When you're still a little kid of seven, someone a year older is practically an adult. He got us into lots of trouble. We lived on a wide leafy street where a lot of the houses were very old. Many of them didn't have garages because they were built before people had their own cars. In Wisconsin this can be a major problem because if the plows come through after a snowstorm and your car is still on the street, you get plowed in. Tony's dad was a radio broadcaster on our public radio station, and that meant he kept an eye on all the forecasts. He made sure his car was facing out in the driveway and that the driveway was clean—Tony had to shovel his share—so all he'd have to do was shovel out the bottom of the driveway after the plow went past.

Tony's dad went on at twelve o'clock noon on the dot and he sometimes didn't get home till nine at night. Anyway, one snow day, which means there was so much snow even the school buses couldn't get through, we got this bright idea of tying our sleds to his bumper. The drifts were so high on either side of the driveway that our sleds were pretty much out of sight. His dad was in a hurry and there wasn't any reason to look behind, so he started the engine and took off. We bumped out of the driveway and skidded across the road as he turned right and then straightened out as the car started uphill. It was a gas! Then another car came up behind us on the steep part and the driver honked and honked till Tony's dad looked in his rearview mirror.

When he got out he said, "You damn fool kids!" so I knew he was pretty mad. He untied the sleds and threw them in the trunk and told us to walk home. He frowned at me and then he said to Tony, "I will deal with you later." I won't tell you what happened after that except to say we missed a whole weekend of perfectly good sledding.

Then there was the day Tony made a bunch of little teepees out of wooden matches, the kind you use to light woodstoves or bonfires, and then he lit a match and held it to the first teepee, which went up so suddenly that he jumped back with a scorched wrist. But Tony's dad didn't think that had taught him enough of a lesson, so he bought a six-pack of those big boxes of matches, 250 matches to a box, and he sat Tony down on the back stoop with a brass plate and he said, "You sit here till you have struck every single match in this six-pack. I want to see every match piled neatly on this tray, understand?"

I can tell you this because I was hiding behind the hedge that separates our backyards.

Tony whined, "But it's suppertime, Dad."

"Well, this is *instead* of supper." And it was.

Tony and I had a clothesline pulley we had rigged up

between our two bedroom windows, only mine was in the bathroom because my bedroom was on the wrong side of the house. In fact, Tony's dad had helped us rig it up. He said he had had one back when he was a kid in Plainfield, New Jersey, where the houses were much closer together and he and his pal used to swap baseball cards that way. Well, I put two candy bars I'd been saving up in the basket and pulleyed them across to Tony that night. So that was his supper. And I didn't get caught.

The other adventure I remember was making our own snuff. We knew smoking tobacco gave you cancer but we figured sniffing it would be okay. Tony said that baseball players did it all the time. Tony's grandfather smoked cigars once a week outside their house, because his grandmother couldn't stand the smell. He kept his supply in a special box. Tony helped himself to one and then he enlisted me to help grind it up. We used my mom's coffee grinder and we ground and ground for about ten minutes, with a couple of cloves in it too for flavor, until the coffee grinder just quit. I said I thought it was tired and needed a rest and we should just get our snuff out and go outside. Which we did. We shook the powder into a little sandwich bag and went out into Tony's yard where there was still a swing set, though everybody had outgrown swinging on it, and we each sat on a swing.

"Who's going first?" Tony said.

"You are, it was your idea."

"No, you should, it was your mom's coffee grinder."

So I did. I took a big pinch of it between my thumb and my first finger the way he said and I stuffed it right up my nose.

"Now sniff!" Tony said.

I sniffed and then I sneezed and then I couldn't stop sneezing and my eyes ran along with my nose, and then I was coughing until my mom came out to see what was going on. I went on coughing and sneezing for about an hour. I'm warning you, stay away from snuff!

The coffee grinder was never the same after that. Mom finally went out and bought a new one, and she took fifty cents a week out of my allowance like almost forever to pay for it. Tony's dad got a better job with a TV station down in Madison and they moved away. I was very sad about that.

But I had a best girlfriend too, back then before my accident. That was Trippy, who you've already met. We were at that age between scuffing around in our mothers' high heels and actually putting on makeup and giggling about boys. Well, I haven't really gotten to that stage yet but my mom says I will. Before I know it I'll get my period and I'll grow breasts, that's what she says. It's funny to remember this now, but I can still see it. In Trippy's room she had a dressing table with a skirt around it and a three-way mirror that stood on it. It never occurred to me how special it was that each of us had our own room. I hadn't found out yet how most of the world lives, and that a lot of people are lucky if there's even one bed for the entire family on a dirt floor. Getting to know Teresa helped me begin to understand how rich we are compared to most of the world. So you might say that I've grown up enough to think about other people's lives but I can't get that dressing table out of my head.

Trippy and I were real tomboys back before my accident. There wasn't anything we couldn't do, like pump the swing so high it looped the loop which was forbidden or climb up to the tree house and then keep on going higher. It was a big copper beech tree with lots of places you could lie back with your feet wedged in a crook and just stay there reading comic books all afternoon. We didn't read comic books though. Back then we were reading the first Harry Potters and then I got onto Doctor Doolittle. That was until I found Jane Goodall and the chimpanzees. I couldn't get enough books about primates in the wild. Even though I was only nine years old I was hooked on saving the environment for wild animals. For instance when we grow up and have kids and our kids have kids they may be the last human beings on Earth to ever see an elephant. Or a polar bear. It is just too sad to think about.

Back in Wisconsin my mom went out on a lot of dates. She didn't call them dates but when the sitter came which was usually one of her students from the university she'd say, "I'm just going out to dinner with some friends, Lisa." (Lisa was my favorite.) "Here's my cell phone number. I'm leaving it on so don't hesitate to call if Lizzie sets the house on fire." This was a favorite joke from Hilaire Belloc. Mom used to read his poems out loud to me at bedtime. "George" was my favorite and his balloon does set the whole house on fire. You should look up his book *Cautionary Tales for Children.*

Her dates were old friends from the university—two professors and one dean—and none of them were father material. Then she met this man who was a writer. He wrote articles for magazines and on the side he was writing a novel. His name was Timothy Shoemaker and I liked him a lot better than the men in the old friends category. He would play hopscotch and statues with me and one rainy day I taught him how to play jacks. We sat on the floor and played onesies and twosies and so on all afternoon. He was fun to be with. Mom seemed to think so too and for a while we saw a lot of Tim. Mom went away with him for a long weekend once. Afterward I asked her was he father material? "Would you marry him?"

She said, "He's not the marrying kind," and changed the subject. I found out way later that there was another woman he went away on long weekends with.

I haven't said yet that I have another friend, he goes to the same school I do and he's smarter than I am. We're both in the eighth grade at Graver Academy, which is a private day school. Mom can afford it because of the settlement. I don't know how much money she got. For one thing, she would never tell me and for another, the settlement says she can't ever say. Josh is a year and a half older than I am. He started school a year late which I'll explain about later, but then he skipped a grade. Because he's a boy his parents wanted him to be in an age-appropriate grade. That's what he told me. I didn't tell him I skipped two. I guess being age-appropriate isn't as important for girls.

I try to do the Sudoku numbers puzzle and the word Jumble in the newspaper every morning before school. I hate it when I get stuck and can't solve one or the other. It practically ruins my day. Mom says I'm an addict—you know, like an alcoholic. Anyway, my chair folds up and it's no trick at all to heave it into the backseat at the last minute for the drive to school.

I found out later that Josh does the Sudoku and the Jumble too.

I asked him, "Don't you hate it when you can't get the numbers to come out right?"

"It's worse when there's a perfectly simple word in the Jumble. I can waste half a pad of paper trying to get *helium,* for instance."

I knew what he meant. "Or even worse, *fedora.*"

Maybe we both read a lot because we're both in wheelchairs. And I love algebra and Latin. They're both so, I don't know how to describe them, I guess I'd say because they're so orderly. I'm taking first-year Latin and it's my favorite subject. Josh is taking it too. Latin just makes better sense than English. If you look at *sink, sank, sunk* or *drink, drank, drunk* you can't help wondering why we have to say *think, thought.* Or *get, got,* or *make, made.* If we say declensions and conjugations it's like we're speaking a secret language. We could make up a code using the cases genitive, ablative, dative to stand for the villains in a mystery story. Let's say Jennifer Genitive has a dog. The eyes of her dog are dark brown. That's the genitive, or possessive, case. Alex Ablative finds some fleas on her dog. The ablative almost always involves a preposition, like *on, to, with,* and so on. Dave Dative forgot to offer food to his dog. *Food* is the direct object and *to his dog* is the indirect. But we agreed that it just gets too complicated to explain if you haven't studied Latin.

CHAPTER 5

I think I already said that Teresa and Digger are just about our best friends here. They live a little way up the beach from us in an apartment their daughter Aurelia found for them. We're next to the right-of-way, which is a path from the street to the beaches. The law says that the beaches belong to everybody, but there are only a few places to get to them from the street and ours is one. We get joggers early in the morning, some of them with dogs, and then later on we get some people who drag in their beach chairs and baby oil and lie down to bake. I feel sorry for them because it has been scientifically proven that all that tanning is bad for you but some people don't know it yet.

Being next to the right-of-way means we can pretty much see every person who comes down the path or walks out on the jetty. Sitting on the back porch gives a pretty good view of any comings and goings. I like to sit there with my binocs—that's what the birder people call them—and check out the shore birds.

One Saturday night Mom and I were watching TV in Teresa and Digger's living room and eating chicken fajitas from these little snack trays Teresa opened out. It seemed we were hanging out there more often than we did in our place. I guess it felt more like home somehow. And the two of them felt so kind of homey to me that I finally asked them if they would be my family.

"You mean like honorary grandparents?" Teresa asked. And I said yes. Then Digger said, "I am honored to be your *abuelito*, Lizzie, *mi amor.*" And Teresa smiled and hugged me so I knew she was now my *abuelita*. So now I had grandparents even if I didn't have a father. That wasn't so special. I knew lots of kids at my old school in Wisconsin who didn't have fathers. Actually, they did have them but the fathers didn't live with them and they only got to see them like every other weekend. I think that is worse than not having any father at all because every time you meet you're like two different people and you have to explain yourself all over again.

There are kids here in my new school who have to spend half their time with their mother and the other half with their father. Or live with their mother and go every other weekend to stay with their father. My friend Josh has two parents who live together, though. I know this because some mornings they're together in the van delivering him, so that pretty much has to mean they spent the night together, doesn't it?

Digger is full of wonderful stories of adventures he had being chief of police.

"Did you have a gun in California?"

"Of course."

"Do you still have it? Can I see it?"

He went in the other room and trotted out with it. It's a

Lizzie! 39

Beretta but it didn't have any bullets in it. "Were there ever any murders in your town?"

He got all solemn and said yes, there had been a terrible one last year before they came east, and he'd solved it but he didn't want to talk about it. I asked Teresa later and she told me it involved a beautiful young woman, but that's all she'd say.

Digger told me about his men's poker group that meets every Tuesday night. "Any money left in the kitty goes to charity."

"Kitty?"

"That's the money on the table from what each man bets."

"But aren't you supposed to win?"

"Yes, *chica,* in a real game. But we only bet for fun."

I was still pretty confused. Like why is it a kitty and not a doggie? But at that point their daughter Aurelia arrived with her live-in boyfriend Tom Rohrsbach. It was the first time we'd met him.

After we shook hands, he said, "What happens when one lion meets another lion? It roars back." I thought that was a lame sort of way to explain how to pronounce his name but I smiled. I don't think he saw me roll my eyes when he turned to say something to Digger. From then on I called him Tom the Lion to myself. Aurelia's nickname is Lia and she's climbing the corporate ladder in finance. That means she's getting to be an important person with lots of people working for her and she travels a lot, which is why she changed her name to Martin.

It's legal to change your name if you're a grown-up. Someday I'd like to change mine to Simone.

"Simone Peterlinz," I say, trying it out loud in private. It sounds sort of mysterious. Lizzie, which stands for Elizabeth, is so plain. Anyway, Lia said Martin was simpler for hotel clerks and for boarding passes but I think Teresa and Digger's feelings were hurt. It was like she was saying she didn't want anybody to know she was Latina. Instead, I think she should be proud of it. You should hear Digger talk about the border fence our country is building.

"My ancestors were living in the US two hundred years ago. They never crossed any border. The border crossed *them.*"

And then he went on to explain about the Mexican-American War that happened before the Civil War. I never knew about that war or the treaty that made Texas and California and so on into states.

Digger's great-great-grandparents practically founded Santa Fe, New Mexico.

"They were living there long before it became a city. So maybe they didn't stand up and announce it but it's where I came from."

If I had Lia's heritage—heritage means what's come down to you from your parents and grandparents and so on—I'd be very proud. My mother's parents are dead and I don't have a father, so it's like I don't have any heritage except for what my mother can tell me. Our last name Peterlinz is most likely German or Austrian, she says, but it goes back about five generations in the US, so she can't tell me much.

Digger's a total insomniac, he just can't sleep. Well, he falls asleep but he's up at three or four a.m. roaming around. He complains a lot about leaving California, but at least Aurelia found them a ground-floor apartment on the ocean, and it's not in a high-rise. "All the snowbirds who live here sit around on their little balconies reading mystery novels till suppertime. Then they all dress up in their party clothes and get in their big old Lincoln Town Cars and drive to a steak house or a seafood place for dinner," Digger says. "They all drive off at seven like a flock of seagulls and they're back with their heads tucked under their wings by ten."

He says he would hate to live on the ninth floor of a modern pink apartment building. He has to be able to open the door and put his feet on the ground. We're lucky to be on a stretch of beach where everything is grandfathered. That means the low-rise buildings and little cottages like ours were built before there were a bunch of rules and nobody can come in and build on top of us.

CHAPTER 6

"Being a feminist doesn't mean you don't like men," Mom said.

She was making pancakes for Trippy and me and we had real maple syrup to put on them. Trippy's mom sent the maple syrup as a house present and we didn't waste any time getting into it.

I had just read the article about Mom in the *Wisconsin Register* that had come in the mail. It said, "Rebecca Peterlinz is a prominent feminist."

"It's not a big deal, Lizzie. It means you believe in equality between men and women in everything. For instance, who gets tenure at the university and who gets elected to Congress shouldn't be based on gender, but on who's best for the job."

"So gender is another way of saying *sex*? Because it sounds better in public? *Sex* just sounds . . . sexy," Trippy said.

Mom laughed. "Good point, Trip. That's why you say *gender politics*. Think if you said sex politics how confused people would be."

And I said, "I'm planning to be a feminist someday too. If only boys weren't such jerks. Please pass the maple syrup."

"Women can be jerks too, Lizzie. The point is equality. You can't discriminate."

After breakfast we were going out with Aurelia and Tom the Lion and Digger and Teresa to watch the parasail competition. They have them every Sunday. This was instead of a date. A week ago, Tom the Lion had said he wanted to fix my mother up with one of his friends on a date and the four of them could go out some evening.

"I don't think so, thanks anyway," my mom said, and she said it as if he had offered to introduce her to a friendly alligator.

So Lia proposed parasailing instead.

"Lizzie and Trippy would love it, Becca." That's what she calls my mom now, which shows the two of them have definitely bonded. *Bonding* is one of those words the school counselor uses during her consultations with my mother. As in I haven't bonded yet with any of the kids at Graver. She didn't know about Josh.

So we did all go, and Tom the Lion's friend that he wanted my mom to meet turned out to be nothing like Tom. Instead, he was more like the Scarecrow in *The Wizard of Oz*, skinny with long arms that he kept folding and unfolding in a raggedy sweater. He had soft brown eyes that were almost too big for his face and enough wrinkles to show he had suffered a lot. Trippy and I found out later that afternoon that his wife had died of cancer two years ago and that she had knitted that sweater. We were eavesdropping on Lia and my mom while we watched all these fantastic guys, and some women too, sort of ski along behind a boat and then be lifted up into the sky by their parachutes and sail until they ran out of wind and came down gracefully. Trippy screamed at the first one. She was sure he would fall down and drown—that's so like Trippy!—but she was loving it.

Most of them glided down safely. A couple did a nose-dive and I was scared too that they were killed, but they came back up to the surface and got hauled into the boat. The winner was supposed to be the skier who had stayed up in the air longest and come down the farthest distance from the starting line. But it was awfully hard to tell who'd gone the farthest because the ocean water never stays still, and even if you put down a marker it can float away.

First prize was two free parasails and the runner-up got one. I guess if you're into parasailing those are good prizes. I was thinking a hundred dollars for a prize would be better but I didn't say it out loud.

After that, we all went to a local fair nearby. It was kind of tacky, with stands selling hot dogs and cotton candy and a midway full of games where if you shot the nose off the picture of a clown's face, you won a prize. The main attraction was the Ferris wheel.

I'd never been up in a Ferris wheel but I didn't want to say I didn't want to go. Somehow, Digger scooped me up and I got paired in one chair with him and my mom and the Scarecrow were in the one in front of us. Lia rode with Tom the Lion and Teresa rode with Trippy. She said she would keep Trippy calm in case we got stuck up in the air. That really scared me but I didn't let on.

Finally all the seats were taken and we began to go up in the sky. Music was playing and people were screaming. I could recognize Trippy's scream. I thought I was going to pass out once we got up to the top because the wheel *did* get stuck, though I found out later that they stop it on purpose on every ride and it was just our luck that Digger and I were at the *apex*—that means at the very top. Then I saw that the Scarecrow had his arm around my mom and she was hiding her head on his chest, so I knew she was just as scared as I was, and for some reason that made me feel better. When we got down, Teresa said, "How does it feel to be back on terra firma? Ready for another ride?"

So I lied and said sure, it was lots of fun but not right now, thank you.

As Digger settled me back down in my wheelchair he whispered, "I was so scared *mi amor*. I was glad I had you to hold onto." That's what he's like, my honorary *abuelo*. Lia and Tom the Lion and the Scarecrow, whose real name I found out is Robert Jacobson—"Call me Rob"—came back to our house afterward. They all sat around on the back porch facing the ocean drinking wine and eating salted peanuts. Trippy and I had orange juice with seltzer water and goldfish crackers while the Scarecrow talked about his recent cases. Turns out he's a partner in a big important law firm in Miami whose clients are mostly white-collar criminals, people who committed fraud or embezzled, both things I had to look up. They're both about ways to steal a lot of money, but not with a gun. But a lot of the Scarecrow's clients are immigrants whose work visas have run out or whose work visas are fake or who never had one in the first place. He can afford to take their cases because of the big-name firm he works for. This is how he explained it.

"Cases where they borrow money to buy a fake work visa and a fake driver's license so they can get a job so they can pay off the man who made the fake visa, but then they can never make enough money to send to their hungry families back home." He also takes juvenile cases, kids under eighteen who've gotten into trouble, and the stories of their lives are so sad.

I never knew how many sad stories there were right here in Florida, never mind in Africa and Afghanistan and so on. Kids in trouble for shoplifting. Burglary. Drugs. Gangs. Even attempted murder and some real murders too.

"A lot of these kids come from broken homes," the Scarecrow said. "Getting into a gang is their way of getting to have a family. And to get in you have to prove yourself."

"How?" I asked him.

"You have to prove how bad you are. So you go along as if it were a joyride. You break a window and enter someone's house while they're away."

"And then what?"

"You grab whatever you think you can sell. Jewelry. Computers. Kitchen stuff, like carving knives. Or you break into a drugstore in the middle of the night and steal some drugs. That's real trouble."

"So how can you help?"

"I can represent them in court. I can advise them beforehand. Sometimes I go visit the family, if there's a family, and get some background."

"And you tell the judge about the background?"

Rob the Scarecrow smiled. He spread his hands out. "Sometimes it can help. It's called *mitigating circumstances.*"

That was another one I was going to look up later.

"He does a lot for those kids," Tom the Lion said. "Everybody in the firm knows he's a soft touch."

I didn't have to ask what a soft touch was. I liked finding out that he had started out as a public defender and he liked working with kids. But I did sort of dream about the Scarecrow and my mom, like maybe if they fell in love they might get married, and then I'd have a real father, not just an intelligent sperm.

Then everybody but Trippy and me went for a walk on the beach to watch the sun go down. That is a favorite activity around here because at the very last minute it's supposed to turn green. Well, greenish.

I said, "I've seen it go down one zillion times, so I'll just stay here and watch the sandpipers."

And Trippy said, "I'll stay with Lizzie." That's what a good friend does.

We took turns with the binocs watching a bunch of sandpipers making a mad dash down to pick up tiny bits to eat before the next wave came in and they skittered up the beach to stay dry. Down and up, down and up, it was really close through my binoculars.

"I don't know how they know," Trippy said. "I mean, when the next wave's coming, so they get to run ahead of it."

"You have to have a sandpiper brain for that." And we laughed.

And then we took turns watching three couples walking into the just-setting sun until they looked like paper silhouettes. I got a really good look at one of those couples, which was my mom and Rob the Scarecrow whose arm was around her, snugged up closer than on the Ferris wheel. And I thought maybe it was close to time for him to kiss her.

CHAPTER 7

om said we could go back to Henry'z Petting Zoo one more time before Trippy had to fly back to Wisconsin. But every day was so full of looking for cool shells for Trippy to take home, and going swimming, floating on our backs and making up stories for each other, and visiting with Teresa and Digger that it turned out there was only one day left.

The next morning we packed a picnic lunch for the three of us and pecans and apple slices for the bears.

Henry was full of smiles when he let us in again.

"It's even better the second time," Trippy said. "I just feel like I've been living here all along. They're both crawling all over me to get at the apple slices."

"And you're not getting nipped?"

"Nope. But I'm careful to watch where their mouths are."

"In the wild, bears eat just about anything, like grubs, grapes, berries, even birds' eggs. Henry feeds them 'bear food.' It looks like dog kibble."

"Maybe it is," Trippy said.

We got out of the bear enclosure and went over to pet the goats.

"Mom says she promised Henry that she'd visit with his

mother. She's going in to have iced tea and whatever, so she asked if we could hang out on our own."

All of a sudden there must have been a little breeze because I heard the same sounds I'd heard once before. I'd asked Henry and he said they were probably birds but he couldn't say for sure because he's a little deaf to begin with.

"Little trills and chucks, I hear them too," Trippy said.

"It must be birds, somebody must be raising birds near here."

"Let's go see."

Trippy wheeled me out past the veggie garden, down through the cornfields. I'd never been out that far. It was neat wheeling down the rows with the cornstalks waving overhead, not knowing when that row would end, and you came out and there was another field and another.

"Are you way tired yet?"

"It's not bad." Trippy was puffing a little. "Listen!"

And then we both could hear the sounds coming steadily, almost like music, a music we'd never heard before. Right in front of us was this big boxy building that looked like an abandoned sugarcane warehouse, not that I've ever seen a sugarcane warehouse.

It wasn't exactly hidden by the live oak trees but it wasn't exactly obvious, either. Kudzu vines grew all over it, making the building look as if it had grown up out of the ground. Kudzu was climbing the surrounding trees too. Sunlight barely filtered through the clearing.

By now we were whispering. "This is spooky," Trippy said.

I wondered what it was for. "Maybe it's a meeting place. Maybe criminals meet here to plot their crimes."

"Lizzie, let's go back! We shouldn't be here, I just know something's gonna happen!"

But by then I had pried away a piece of rotted wood and found a sort of slit. I bent down low in my chair so I could look through.

What I saw in there blew my mind.

"Well, what is it? What's in there?"

"Shh. Here, bend down and look. Quick!"

Trippy wheeled me just far enough from the open slit so that she could take my place.

Then she put her hands over her whole face and stood up. "Oh my God, what are they?"

"Some kind of little monkey. They have to be monkeys with those tails."

"But all that golden fur! Who's ever heard of monkeys that color?"

"I don't know. And I've never seen monkeys that tiny."

"Maybe they're here on loan from some zoo," Trippy said.

"Maybe." I didn't want to say so right there but I knew I was looking at a crime.

"Come on, let's get out of here. This place gives me the creeps." Trippy was really jittery.

"Me too. I'm pretty sure we're on somebody else's land and we might get in trouble for trespassing, so let's not mention where we've been."

"Okay."

There was a little shack across the way we hadn't noticed at first and suddenly this tall skinny guy came out. When I looked closer I could see he was still a kid but a lot older than we were. When he saw us he threw his hands up like we were the FBI or something and then he sort of realized we weren't there to arrest him. So he reached out his hand to shake mine and said, "*Hola*. My name is Julio." And I said, "Happy to meet you, my name is Lizzie. And this is my friend Trippy."

"*Hablas español?*" he asked, and I told him I knew only a little. He used a combination of Spanish and English and some sign language to tell us he worked in the building and he also tended the cornfields and yes, he was the one who weeded the vegetables and picked cucumber beetles and potato bugs off the plants early every morning. That figured, because I didn't think Henry the Huge could do all that. I asked him where he lived and he pointed off to one side under the live oaks to the shack that might have been a storage shed or henhouse once.

By now Trippy had pressed both hands over her mouth as if to say she couldn't believe this was happening—and to tell the truth, neither could I. He saw the look of surprise on my face and he said, "I know, it's not much, but I live there for free." What he really said was half in Spanish but I understood what he meant—"*Mi casita no es gran cosa, lo sé*"—and then he said it all in English. His English sounded perfectly good to me but he acted like he wasn't quite comfortable with it.

We didn't dare stay any longer, so I gestured to show we were going back through the fields, but before we left he put his fingers to his lips and said, "Secret. Promise?" which he then said over again as "*No digas nada, ¿me prometes?*" I nodded and held my right hand over my heart to show I promised and Trippy did the same thing. My heart was beating so fast that it felt like I had just run the hundred-yard dash back when my legs could work and Trippy turned my chair around and we headed back. Trippy wheeled me most of the way and then I wheeled myself the rest, so it would look normal.

Mom was coming out of Henry's house as we came around the garden. Our timing was terrific. And just as we were getting ready to leave, Jeb Blanco's Learjet swooped down, so we had to stay for that. We watched it land a long way away on Henry's cow pasture. And right on time the Lincoln Navigator came whizzing up Henry's road and drove out to the plane. Pretty soon Jeb Blanco came driving back and this time the same two men were in the backseat.

He got out of the car and greeted Mom and me as if we were his long-lost friends. We *observed the amenities*—that's what Mom calls it—and said we were fine and how was he and then I introduced Trippy and then Henry joined us.

Jeb Blanco said, "Ah, *hola*, Henry. I'm glad you're here today because I found the names of some greens that I know will grow here for you," and he took out a little red leather notebook. "I'm going to write these down and then we'll have to see where we can buy the seeds to try them out." He patted his shirt pocket, his suit pocket, his back pockets, then he said, "I think I must have left my pen in the plane."

I reached into the little case that's attached to the right arm of my chair and held a ballpoint out to him.

"Ah, good! Thank you." He turned sideways to lean the notebook on the hood of the car, then printed in very precise capital letters MALABAR SPINACH, NEW ZEALAND SPINACH, and BATAVIAN LETTUCE and tore the page out. I could see Henry's lips moving as he read the words. Then he folded the page in half and slipped it into his shirt pocket. I felt Trippy nudging me. She was nodding at Jeb Blanco and wiggling her left hand so I knew she was telling me he was one of her clan. I found out a long time ago that only about ten percent of people are left-handed. Trippy is one of them and she sort of collects other lefties but I didn't think she would mention this to Blanco. I was right. And then I had to open my big mouth.

"I think I remember where I saw you, Mr. Blanco."

"Really, *pequeñita*? Tell me."

"It was on the jetty out past where we live in Woodvale. Practically right next to where the cruise ships leave? I think I saw you walk out there one time. Or maybe a couple of times."

He acted puzzled. "Woodvale? I don't believe I have ever been there."

"Wasn't it you walking with your briefcase past our cottage, down the right-of-way? I thought I saw you out there talking to one of the fishermen."

He threw his head back and laughed. "Last week someone claimed he knew me in Atlanta. The week before that somebody in Philadelphia swore I was his second cousin and now I am in . . . where did you say you live?"

"Woodvale." But by now I was feeling embarrassed.

"Right. Woodvale, where I have never been. Well, how would you like a ride in my plane, *pequeñita*? You and your little friend here? The next time I come to see Henry and his poor mama."

I murmured something about how that would be nice.

But what I was really thinking was that I wouldn't go up in his plane with him if he offered me a million dollars.

CHAPTER 8

I hated to see Trippy go back to the frozen north the next day, but at the same time I was worried. Here we were walking around with a deep secret and I was scared neither of us would be able to hold it in much longer. Trippy swore with a "cross my heart and hope to die" swear that she would be faithful to our secret but I knew how tempted she'd be to tell the whole story.

I said, "I think we better encrypt the monkeys in our emails. How about if we call them 'the goldfinches'?"

"That's a great idea! I'm going to start looking them up as soon as I get home."

How long could Trippy last? For that matter, how long could I? And then I started thinking about Josh. If I had to spill the beans I felt he was the one friend I could trust. We're a lot alike. Josh's whole name is Joshua Blaine. A lot of the other kids kind of snicker when he answers a question because when he gets excited and raises his hand it sort of flaps, and if Mr. Hammersmith catches them making *derogatory* (look it up) sounds, he gives them detention. Well, let them be jerks if they want to. Josh has a nifty electric wheelchair and his mom drives a van with a side door and a ramp so he can roll himself in and out on his own. I know this because our moms turned out to be *alumnae* of the same college. They both went to Wellesley, which is in Massachusetts, but they didn't know each other there. Josh's mother is five years older.

"So how do you say it," I asked him, "is it *alumn-eye* or *alumn-knee*?"

"Well, it turns out people say it either way, but the 'eye' ending is the right one because it's the plural of *alumna*."

"For a guy it would be *alumnus*, right?"

"Yep. And here's where it gets tricky. The plural is *alumni*, with an *i*. It should be pronounced 'knee,' but almost everybody who hasn't taken Latin says 'eye.' For some reason this cracked me up and then Josh cracked up too.

This was over lunch. Then out of the blue, I invited him to come home with me the next afternoon. Of course my mom thought it was a great idea since I hadn't been exactly eager to invite anyone from Graver. "I thought you hated everybody at school."

"Well, apparently not."

"When were you thinking?"

"How about tomorrow?"

"I'll call his mother," Mom said, and it was settled.

It wasn't exactly a surprise but more of a relief when Josh accepted. The next day I couldn't wait for school to let out. As soon as I got home I waited out front for Josh. But I didn't want it to appear obvious that I was waiting for him so I wheeled up to Mom's plantings of petunias, which are a pain in the neck to keep watered but they do bloom a lot. I sort of leaned forward and acted busy deadheading them until I heard an approaching vehicle. Josh's mom was driving. Anyway, I did what Mom taught me to do. I *observed the amenities* and introduced myself.

And then his mother said, "Hi, Lizzie. I'm Josh's mom. Please call me Jenna."

I said, "Would you like to come in and meet my mom?" but just then my mom appeared, and the two of them stood outside talking, so that was taken care of. Josh and I wheeled up the ramp into our house and of course after Jenna drove off Mom asked us if we'd like anything to eat, like grapes or tangerines and oatmeal cookies. After pigging out we went into the study where my computer is. It used to be my mom's and we sort of shared it but then she got a new one. So now this is my own Mac and it does everything but talk. After a few minutes Mom called in to say she was going down to the beach to catch a swim, did we want to come?

"I think we'll hang out here. I'm going to show Josh some of the stuff on my computer."

After I heard the door close I swore Josh to everlasting secrecy, even under torture or in *durance vile*, like in the Middle Ages, and then I described what I'd seen in the warehouse. "Little monkeys—at least thirty of them all in cages, about six or eight to a cage—all swinging on the bars and climbing all over each other on these big tops of trees someone had put in, and curling up in these wicker baskets that were tied to the treetops, and keeping up this constant sort of chuckling and trilling.

"I couldn't tell whether it was a distress call or just their way of communicating. They're beautiful, Josh. They have these—I don't know what to call them—manes, I guess, all silky yellow."

"Let's Google them," Josh said, and we did. There were about twenty entries for *small monkeys* and after we browsed through them all we printed out a promising one.

"'Golden lion tamarins,'" I read. Josh had wheeled in so close to me that I could smell the freshly ironed smell of his shirt and our wheels were in danger of locking but I didn't care. "'Slightly smaller than squirrels. They are about twelve inches tall, not including the tail, and can weigh up to two pounds.'" We learned all sorts of facts. Like when they mate, the mother always has twins. The father stays around to help take care of them and he often carries the babies on his back. They live in the rain forests of Brazil and they are endangered because farmers are clearing the rain forests to make room to grow crops for their families. The tamarins have lost 95 percent of their natural habitat.

"Well, if they're endangered, whoever's importing them is breaking the law."

"Big time," I agreed. "But who do you suspect is smuggling them? And how? It can't be Henry. And I'm pretty sure it can't be the older kid we met, the one who takes care of them and swore us to secrecy. He looked pretty scared himself."

"What about the guy you were telling me about—the guy you met that day with your mother?"

"Jeb Blanco, that's what he says to call him. His whole name is Jesús Ernesto Blanco."

"Right. Let's Google him."

There were thirty-four hits for *Jesús Ernesto Blanco*. One was a convicted felon from Colombia. Another was a prize-fighter in Texas. Another was the owner of a grocery store in Nebraska who was accused of swiping produce at night from a market chain to sell in his store. Another was a hero for performing the Heimlich maneuver on a diner who was choking at a neighboring table at La Zesta somewhere in Manhattan, and so on.

"Wait a minute!" said Josh. "I bet this is our guy: 'Jesús Ernesto Blanco, owner of Imp-Ex, a major import and export firm with headquarters in New York City, has recently acquired Miami Flash, an importing nexus for rare objects from around the globe. Two years ago, Miami Flash was indicted for illegally importing three orangutans, ostensibly intended for zoos in St. Louis, Denver, and Seattle. An alert customs agent is credited with discovering the animals in a shipment of teak lumber; one of the orangutans was dead and the other two were in respiratory distress. Miami Flash stock tumbled and the firm barely averted bankruptcy.'"

"Wow! First orangutans, now tamarins. This guy is a major, major criminal."

"But what does *indicted* mean? And what's a *nexus*?"

"When in doubt look it up," Josh said. So we did.

I also looked up *ostensibly* without telling him because I wasn't sure. Three new words in an afternoon—not bad.

We got off Google then because we could hear my mom coming back. I didn't have to ask Josh to keep my secret. He got the picture.

"Can Josh stay for supper?" I asked her. She said sure, if he phoned his mother and she okayed it.

We talked about a lot of things during supper—spaghetti and meatballs, which Josh said was his favorite meal—stuff we might never have gotten to if we hadn't been sitting across from each other at our kitchen table, not the hideously noisy cafeteria at Graver. We said a lot more about where we were with our bum legs. Josh *can* walk. Sort of, as he put it. He uses his chair at school because he doesn't want to have the whole student body watch him *gimp-and-gallump* from place to place. I knew just what he meant. I can sort of walk too, though with me it's more like *clip-clop-flop*. It's humiliating to do it on two quad canes in front of a whole cast of normals, and my legs are only good for four or five steps, like from chair to couch. And don't tell me to exercise. Believe me, you people reading this don't know Day One about exercise. I've done at least a million push-pulls. I've stepped a million steps between the parallel bars.

Mom would say, "Lizzie, I've told you a million times not to exaggerate." And then we'd both laugh.

Mom came up with ice cream and brownies from somewhere for dessert—she is just a magician when it comes to putting a supper together out of odds and ends. Then she left us and went out on the porch to read one of her academic journals. We kept on talking.

Josh's favorite subject is history but he's like me, he'll read anything.

"The back of a box of cereal, ads for life insurance, whatever," he said.

He says he averages about three books a week, pretty much like me. He reads a lot about the civil rights movement. I'm more into Jane Goodall and saving the habitat for animals. I already told you that he does the Sudoku and Jumble puzzles every day, which made it clear to me that we were meant for each other. For fast friends, I mean. I wasn't thinking anything, you know, sexy. And he has an older brother Greg, who's a senior at Graver, but I haven't met him so far. Turns out he's been in Italy for three weeks with his Advanced Latin class. Is that ever boss? The sweet thing is that he has his own car. Josh says it's a real junker but it runs and sometimes he can get Greg to drive him places but then he has to go on his canes.

Then we got to talking about our "conditions." That's Josh-talk for what the doctors say when you have to go for a checkup, as in "given your condition" . . . and he asked me what I remembered about hitting my head. "I remember racing out onto the board and slipping and thinking, uh-oh, something bad is about to happen. But I swear I have *perfect amnesia* for the rest. You read about characters in books having perfect amnesia and then I had it and it was true. I didn't remember anything until I woke up in the hospital around midnight that night."

"Wow. So you were unconscious for what—about twelve hours?"

"Something like that. Everything was hushed with no overhead lights on and I didn't know where I was. I just knew I had this horrible headache. It was so scary because I was connected to all these . . . apparatuses dripping stuff into me and measuring my heartbeat and pulse and beeping. I was so confused. I knew I wasn't dead because the machine was beeping but I think I must have cried out because then my mom woke up—she had been dozing in a chair next to my bed. My head hurt so bad it was unbelievable, and they said I couldn't have any painkillers until they found out, and I quote, *the extent of the damage.*"

"Gross," Josh said.

"Yep, and the next day was awful. I had to have all these scans where they make you lie flat and they slide you into a machine like a coffin and then you really do think maybe you've died until you come out the other end."

"So did you, like, fracture your skull?"

"Absolutely. I came down on the back of my head. And mashed my spinal cord which is why I'm . . . well, you know." I drummed on the arms of my chair a few times to sort of ease the tension I could feel building up in the room.

Then Josh did this incredible thing. He reached over and took hold of my hand and squeezed it.

I squeezed back and then he let go.

Then I showed Josh my *American Heritage Dictionary.* You can find anything you want on the web just as fast but I like turning real pages. I flipped to the d's and scanned down to *diplegia,* which is what he has. It comes from the Latin *plangere*, to strike. Just so you'll know, it means paralysis of matching parts on both sides of the body. The reason he started school late was because he was having surgery for it. He's had three operations so far.

Then Josh told me some of the background to his diplegia.

"I was a preemie. A premature baby, nobody knows why. Mom says I only weighed two and a half pounds when I was born. I had some trouble breathing in the beginning but I outgrew that. They say that a lot of the kids with diplegic CP may have some learning problems but my only problem is learning when to shut up in class."

We both laughed at that. "And eventually I'm going to

be able to walk almost normally, though right now I'm just fighting off some knee and ankle problems."

"But See Pee, what's that?"

"It stands for cerebral palsy."

I felt stupid not to know that, but Josh didn't seem to notice.

He told me about his PT sessions every week and that they were painful because his muscles had shortened and it would take a long time to get them to lengthen and get stronger.

"Boy, can I relate to that! My PTs just about killed me with all their pushing and pulling me. But Mom says they saved my leg muscles and that's why I need to keep doing these crummy exercises every single day. Even though I'm never going to walk, really walk, it's important to save every little bit of muscle I've got. That's so I can sit up straight and make all these transfers, in and out of cars, out of this chair and into the ocean. You know. I'm supposed to practice getting up with my quad canes every day too, but sometimes I just don't . . . have time."

"You're supposed to *make* time," Josh said sternly.

"You too, buddy."

And we high-fived each other.

CHAPTER 9

I somehow got through the next few days in a fog. My heart was heavy from carrying around my big secret. And then, one night, Mom and I ended up going out to eat with my honorary grandparents.

Digger said he loved Thai food and there was a little hole-in-the-wall Thai restaurant hardly anybody else knew about in Woodvale. Teresa found it the first week they moved in and they'd been going there about once a week ever since. Lucky for me there weren't any stairs and nobody acted surprised to see somebody in a wheelchair. The Martinezes were patted and exclaimed over in Thai because they went there so often, and we were given a very warm greeting too. They took away one chair and wheeled me into place with a flourish. Everybody else had beer. I guess it's sort of a tradition to order Thai beer to go with the spicy food. I got a ginger ale. It came with a section of orange on the rim and a red cherry floating on top of the drink, which made it the most unusual ginger ale I ever drank.

Teresa and my mom were deep in conversation about a community action project to provide activities for the immigrant children whose parents were fruit pickers not far from Woodvale, so I had a chance to talk to Digger sort of alone. I took a deep breath and began. "Digger, I have to tell you something only my friends Trippy and Josh and I know, and even Josh hasn't seen it firsthand."

"Your secret is safe with me, *angelita*," and he sort of crossed his eyes in a joking way.

"No, this is really something dangerous. Something I saw at Wilderwood last time while Mom went into Henry's house to check on his mom because she never comes out."

"Whoa. Slow down, *chiquita*. Wildwood? What is it?"

"Wilderwood. It's where there's a petting zoo. Mom drives me there once a week. Henry, who owns it—well I think he owns it, but he may be giving it to this other rich man we met—he has two orphan bear cubs and I get to go in their space and play with them. I get to carry them around with me in my chair, or I used to, but now they're too big to cuddle and he's going to take them off somewhere and probably shoot them to get rid of them. But that's not the secret part."

Right about then Teresa and Mom finished their conversation. The food came and we all started to eat. Everybody had ordered something different so we'd all have a chance to taste all the dishes. Luckily, Thai people use forks and spoons and not chopsticks or I would have been in a pickle. There was a ton of rice and almost too much food to finish. I did taste everything, though I probably wouldn't have, except we were in a restaurant with our sort of still-new friends who were now my honorary grandparents, and I was the only kid. I would have been embarrassed not to but frankly, I wish I could have had a slice of pizza instead.

But Teresa hadn't forgotten what I was telling Digger. "What's this about who's shooting what?"

So then I had to start over about Henry. Mom says he has country ways and she doesn't think he would shoot the bear cubs. It's just part of his act, his bluster, she calls it.

"He's not really running a zoo. There's hardly anybody else who comes there except Mom and me. Does this mean he'll get into trouble about the cubs?"

The grown-ups agreed it was a shame. Fish and Wildlife would have to be alerted. My mom said, "Henry needs guidance, but he's somewhat limited mentally." And the three of them agreed they would make an effort to deal with this matter without Henry being taken to court.

I caught hold of Digger's shirtsleeve and pinched him hard enough so he flinched and turned toward me. "I have to talk to you." He caught on. "I'm taking Lizzie into the kitchen to meet Arun and his wife," he told Teresa. After he wheeled me in and introduced me, we shook hands all around. They smiled and made little bows with their hands folded pointing up in a churchly way and went back to the stove where several pans were sizzling. "Okay. Now tell me."

"But what about—?"

"Arun and Siriket? They won't be able to follow what we say."

So then I told him about the big warehouse and the tamarins I saw in cages. I barely mentioned the big skinny kid who told us to go back the way we came.

He whistled. "*¡Madre mía!* Are you sure?"

"Cross my heart and hope to die."

"How many would you guess?"

I tried to think. Their little golden heads flashed and blurred in my brain. "Maybe thirty or forty?"

Digger frowned. "Lizzie, this is too big to keep secret. We need to notify the police."

"But wait! Henry is friends with this rich guy. I think they're friends, though maybe Henry just works for him. His name is Jeb Blanco and Josh and I Googled him and found out—"

"Slow down, slow down, *chica*. Jeb is a name?"

"It's short for Jesús Ernesto Blanco. That's what we Googled and we found out he owns a company called Imp-Ex—it stands for import and export—get it?"

"And how do you know he's a rich guy?"

"He has his own private plane, it's a Learjet and he lands it on a dirt strip out in Henry's cow pasture."

"And so you think he's bringing in these tiny little monkeys you saw."

"Well, they had to get there somehow."

Digger said, "They could have come by boat also. We'll have to find out."

"But what do you suppose he's planning to do with them?"

"I'm not sure. Anything he does with them is illegal unless he has a permit to import them, which I doubt. I do know there are some fancy people in Hollywood and Reno and Las Vegas and so on who will pay a lot of money. Tens and tens of thousands to have a little tamarin as a pet."

"But they're a very . . . social species, they can't be separated just like that. They would die of loneliness!"

Digger sighed. "*Chica*, there are crazy people who have leopards for house pets. Pumas and jaguars, you name it. And they pay a lot of money, like half a million dollars just to have an exotic animal to call their own."

I looked at him. I couldn't say anything because I was trying so hard not to cry, just thinking about the tamarins so busy in their cages, climbing up and down and trilling and chuckling to each other and curling up in a group to nap in the wicker baskets and then to be taken out and stuffed in a bag of some sort and flown to a rich person's mansion and probably put in a cage all alone. "*Chiquita*, this could be a nasty business. We need to call the police before somebody gets hurt."

"Oh please, Digger. Think if you break this case open what a big story it will make! Please, please figure out a way to drive out there with me just once."

CHAPTER 10

This is going to be a very short chapter. I asked Mom if she thought it was possible to love and hate someone at the same time. She said yes, of course it was. "That's what we call mixed feelings, Lizzie. There's a word for feeling that way, *ambivalence*."

Of course I looked it up and no surprise, it comes from the Latin *ambi,* meaning both sides and *valeo,* strength or vigor. To feel strongly two ways at the same time is exactly what is going on inside me.

I am strongly ambivalent about Henry the Huge. I love him for running his petting zoo where he feeds his animals every day and gives them freshwater whenever they need it and makes sure they have shelter from the sun when it's burning down on them and from the rain when it pours. Especially I love him for looking after the bear cubs. I love his vegetable garden, though I know he doesn't work in it even if he pretends to.

But then I hate him for having those bear cubs at all. They don't belong in a roadside petting zoo. I don't know how he got them but I'm sure he didn't just find them lost in the woods. I hate him for being friends with Jeb Blanco. There is something spooky about Jeb Blanco. I hate that every time Henry's cat has kittens he drowns them in a pail of water. This last time, though, Mom got him to let her take them to the SPCA after they were weaned. That's how I got Tigger. And then we took the mama cat to the vet to be spayed. Guess who paid for it? Right.

To be honest, I have a bunch of other ambivalent feelings. I love my mother but sometimes she makes me so mad that I wheel into my room and slam the door as hard as I can, which isn't very hard because I have to turn my body halfway around to reach the doorknob, and then to give it a real whack I have to stop and lock my wheels or I'll skid forward into my dresser. Usually it's over doing my exercises or not wanting to go down to the beach or why do we have to have macaroni and cheese again.

I'm mixed up about myself too. Most of the time I'm perfectly happy being left alone so I can read or look up words to find out where they come from or work on this autobiography. Some days I think I'm going to become a professional writer and write my own column in a major newspaper and answer all the letters people send me. There will be more letters than Dear Abby gets and I'll have to hire someone to help me keep up. Some days I miss my old life and my old friends from before the accident so bad that I just want to go back to bed and cry. I have days when I feel so lonely that all I want to do is lie down and weep like somebody in Louisa May Alcott but I try not to let anybody know it.

CHAPTER 11

The next morning while I was eating my cereal and bananas, Digger called Mom. He said he had dialed the wildlife emergency hotline about the bear cubs last night. He told them he was retired Chief of Police Diego Martinez from Montandino, California, and they were very interested. They asked him to check out the situation and report back. So he would be making a separate trip to the petting zoo today on his own. I knew it wasn't just about the cubs. I felt like somebody who got all dressed up for the party and then didn't get invited. I didn't even finish my cornflakes. By the time Mom dropped me off at school I was in a bad mood. Right in the middle of algebra class the principal sent for me. I hadn't done anything wrong that I could think of but I wheeled down to the office with a sinking feeling in my stomach.

"It's nothing bad, Lizzie," the secretary told me. "There's a message from your mom that a man named Diego Martinez will be picking you up after school today. He'll have to sign in. We have to be very careful about strangers, you understand. Do you know who he is? Is that going to be all right?"

I knew she meant that any stranger is a security issue.

You can't just drop in at Graver Academy, so I said, "He's my honorary grandfather, he's a very important man. And it's very all right." But now I was all confused. If Digger was going to investigate Henry and the cubs this morning, why was he coming to get me after school this afternoon? And where was Mom going to be? I hope I remembered to say thank you before I went back to class. Graver is big on manners. At lunch I just had time to tell Josh where Digger had gone this morning and how confused I was that he was coming to get me after classes.

He agreed. "But you'll see. There's bound to be a reason." Then the bell rang. "Catch up with you later." Digger met me at Graver and there was a reason. It turned out that Henry had called Mom just after she took me to school. He'd asked her for a favor. Would she come and get him and drive him and his mother to the hospital in Dirk Isle? His mother's legs were very swollen and he'd finally convinced her that she needed to see a doctor. Of course Mom said yes.

"So who's going to take care of the animals?" I asked Digger.

"We are, *chica.*"

With that, I cheered up. Feeding the animals was super easy and it would be fun to show off for Digger. Kibble for Buddy and Blossom. Hay for the goats and burro. Chicken-scratch feed for the fowl and two or three lettuce leaves for the iguana and tortoise, if they were interested.

Henry had left the key to the bears' enclosure under the yellow brick, as promised. I felt very proud as I unlocked the gate and Digger came in with me to admire Buddy and Blossom.

"*Chica*, I have a confession to make. I have never been this close to a bear before," he said as he doled out pecans one after the other. "This is my first and probably my last time."

After we'd fed all the animals, Digger helped me back in the car. We didn't turn left where we usually do. Instead, we went right past the HENRY'Z sign. "According to my GPS there has to be a little road about half a mile from here," Digger said. In case you don't know about GPS, that's Global Positioning Something, go look it up, because a lot is happening these days when it comes to directions.

And there was a little road. It was dirt, no sign.

"This looks hopeful," Digger said. We went slowly around one bend and then another and there was the old wooden warehouse so overgrown with kudzu that it could have been mistaken for an enormous thicket. Just as we pulled over, a tall skinny kid came out—the same shy one Trippy and I had met.

I leaned out the window and said, "*¡Hola!*" He jumped about a mile and looked like he was about to take off like a scared rabbit. Then he recognized me.

"*¡Hola!* You're Lizzie, right? *Te llamas Lizzie, ¿no?*"

"Yes, and this is my honorary grandfather, Diego Martinez. He's a chief of police."

Julio looked terrified. "But you promised me . . . *Pero me prometiste. . . .*"

"No, no, he's a retired chief from California and he's a good person, he's a friend."

"Is there somebody else coming too?"

"No. We came alone. My mom came early this morning to drive Henry and his mother to the hospital."

"Well, you're too late. *Llegaron demasiado tarde.* They're all gone. *Ya se fueron todos.*"

Then Digger said, "What's all gone? Who are you? Do you work here?"

"My name is Julio Blanco. *Trabajo aquí.* I do all the work, I looked after the monkeys from the day Jeb brought them."

I gasped. "Are you related to Jeb Blanco?"

"He's my uncle. *Es mi tío.*"

"So you're saying you work for him?"

"I don't want to, believe me. But what can I do? I broke out of juvie and had no place to go. *No tengo casa.*"

I said, "What's *juvie*? What's that got to do with the monkeys?"

"Lizzie, you don't know how it is, living on the street, *en la calle*. I never knew from one day to the next where I'd eat, where I'd spend the night, where I'd end up. That's why I'm here."

"I get it now," I said. "You're the one who weeds the garden, you keep everything watered, you mulch the plants. I didn't think Henry could do that all by himself."

"Right. I do the garden. And until yesterday I did all this." He gestured to the now silent warehouse. "My uncle and his helpers came for the monkeys. *Todos los monos.* Stuffed them all into two bags and took off. Left two dead ones on the floor."

"Hold on here," Digger said. "This uncle of yours, Jeb, and his whatever-you-call-them, his accomplices, took the monkeys and what?"

"Jammed them into his jet and flew out of here, *en su avión.* I don't know where they were taking them, I just know there was a big fight about money. Not with this one guy Oskar, but with the guy who brings them in by boat."

"You know all this?"

"Well, I'm not part of anything that goes on. I just work here for barely enough to pay for my groceries. My uncle is hiding me. *Mi tío me esconde.* If I don't do what he says he'll either turn me over to the gang or take me back to juvie."

I asked, "Why were you in juvie?"

"I was the lookout."

"Lookout? What were you looking out for?" But then Digger took Julio by the elbow and walked him away from the car. I knew I had asked too many questions.

Now I couldn't hear what they were saying but I knew they were rattling away in Spanish. After a while they walked back and Digger came over.

"I'm going in for a minute, *angelita*. I'll be right back."

It was no use saying I want to come too, so I just nodded. I could see a little shack across the road. Probably that was where Jeb Blanco had been hiding Julio. But it was frustrating not knowing the whole story.

They were gone quite a while. I heard them talking but as soon as they came close to the car, they stopped. Digger looked very grim.

To my astonishment Julio was coming with us. "Where are you taking him? Are you taking him to jail?"

"No, *chica*. I am taking him to be placed in protective custody. I am going to keep him in a separate location until we can get a lawyer to untangle this mess."

"Rob the Scarecrow? The lawyer who works in the same office as Lia's boyfriend?"

"Very possibly Robert Jacobson will take the case. Until then, Lizzie, I am swearing you to secrecy."

"Yes, but tell me . . ."

"Raise your right hand and swear."

"I do, I do! Now tell me."

"It's privileged information, *chiquita*. I can't tell you."

"Not anything about his background, like his place of birth and so on?"

Digger look very grave. "No, *mi amor*, not even that."

On the drive back to Woodvale nobody spoke. It was eerie, like someone had died. I found out later that Digger had examined the two dead tamarins on the floor of the warehouse. Julio told him he thought they died from fright when Jeb and his buddies were stuffing them into burlap bags to take them to the plane. They were probably the same two men who drove the car out to meet Blanco's plane every time he landed in Henry's cow pasture.

Digger took me to our cottage and waited until I had gotten in. Two minutes after he drove away with Julio, Mom returned. She was very cheerful. "Guess what? The doctor in the emergency room was very nice and we didn't have to wait very long at all. He put Henry's mother on a diet for her blood pressure and ordered medication for her swollen legs and Henry has a number to call to tell the doctor how she is doing.

A miracle," Mom said, rolling her eyes, and I knew she was remembering what we went through after my accident. Just thinking the word *hospital* makes me smell it all over again, the ironing-board smell like when a shirt is being pressed, the fresh-scrubbed smell that pricks your eyes open when they push your bed down the hallway as the lights go by overhead. Two weeks in the ICU on a rotating bed. Two more weeks in the neuro unit. Three weeks in the rehab hospital. I don't usually let myself go back to those times. There were a lot of days when all I wanted to do was sleep. But that doesn't work in a rehab hospital. In rehab they are waking you up all the time to go to PT. You have to get up into a sitting position, you have to learn how to transfer to a wheelchair by sliding onto a board and then sliding from the board to the chair. When your arms get strong enough, you can transfer just using your deltoids and pectorals—or whatever they're called—without any board. I was terrible at it at first. I cried a lot in the beginning. Now it's easy.

Sometimes I still cry in secret, though and a lot of it is about how good my mom was to me. How the accident was my own fault for being in such a hurry to show off and now I would have to pay for it the rest of my life. And even though I say I don't care about not having a father, I sometimes cry about that too.

Mom took leave from her teaching job at the university and came to stay with me every single day. She brought piles of books on my favorite subjects—horses and exotic animals and one by one the Harry Potter books. When I didn't feel like reading myself she'd read to me. She was always upbeat.

Even before we got back to Woodvale that day I could see that Digger was different now. He was still my grandfather but suddenly he had turned very professional. He had morphed into the tight-lipped chief of police.

While Mom was still chatting with Digger I rolled up to

my computer and hit my emails. I had to let Trippy in on the latest events, but at the same time I was sworn to secrecy by Digger. I decided to tell her that "the goldfinches" turned out to be very valuable birds that had been stolen and now they were gone, but I left out the rest of the story about Digger and Julio and that he was being *placed in protective custody*. "I swore an oath to Digger that I wouldn't tell anything about Julio yet," I wrote. "More info tomorrow."

I could see Trippy practically hopping up and down not knowing what else was happening but I couldn't help it. Once you raise your right hand and swear, an oath is an oath.

CHAPTER 12

Well, I know this sounds crazy with so much happening almost at once, but believe it or not, there was a murder practically in front of our cottage! Digger was the one who discovered it. It was the very next morning. He'd had insomnia again and he got up at four a.m. and puttered around and finally he pulled on a sweatshirt and went for a walk on the beach barefoot. Teresa is always after him to take walks. I remember the first day Mom and I met them on the beach, Digger wiggled his toes and said, "When I was a kid I never wore shoes except to school. And now after six months of going barefoot my feet are feeling young again."

It was just as Mom was starting to get supper ready that Digger and Teresa stopped by our cottage. Digger told us in great detail everything that had happened, starting at four o'clock that morning.

"It was still dark but you could see the horizon line," he began. "The tide was coming in and I sort of splashed through it. I was feeling pretty good for an old retired chief of police with a bad heart, and I watched the sky show streaks of pink and yellow as I walked. You know about the jetty?"

I said, "It's practically in front of our cottage and I sometimes see people who come out to fish from it." I was remembering when Mom first got me this neat little pair of binocs so I could watch the shorebirds, of which there are many, and try to match them up with the pictures in *Birds of Florida*. So far I've learned to tell an ibis from an egret and not a whole lot more. I use them to people-watch too. Sometimes I can see somebody—usually a man but sometimes a woman—catch a fish and haul it in and drop it into their pail. Once there was this enormous skate, like a black kite. I could see them holding it up for everyone to admire. Little speedboats zoom around the jetty too. And twice, just as it was getting really dark, I got to see a man walk a long way out on the jetty and then another man give him something. I couldn't see exactly what it was.

But I needed to listen to what Digger was saying. "The jetty is where I try to walk to every morning—it's about half a mile away. You know, they made that jetty about thirty years ago. They dredged up those big rocks piled there to make the channel wide enough for all the cruise ships."

I said, "Mom and I always go outside just before dark whenever a cruise ship is starting out. 'Setting sail' is what they call it, though they don't hoist any sails anymore because they have big engines."

I wanted to describe how each ship is about as long as a city block and every deck is all lit up like they're having a permanent New Year's Eve party. When they go through the channel they hoot their horns and that deep-throated sound always makes me shiver. Every cruise ship has to take a pilot along to navigate through the channel—it's the law—

and then when the water is deep enough, a tender comes alongside to bring the pilot back to the harbor. But this wasn't the time. I had to pay attention to Digger.

"When I got there I saw someone out on the very end of the jetty. At first I thought he was fishing. He didn't move at all, so I thought maybe he'd fallen asleep. With the tide coming in, I thought he'd wake up pretty soon or else he was going to get very wet."

"Was that a dead body? I bet it was."

"Hold on, Lizzie. I'm getting to that. Well, I picked my way out there along the sandy strip between the rocks to see if I knew this guy and when I got there I saw his throat had been cut. The blood wasn't running down him anymore but the whole front of him was the reddish brown of dried blood, so I knew he'd been dead for a while."

He paused for a moment. "Thing was, I had my flashlight but I'd forgotten my cell phone." He turned to Teresa and said, "I knew you'd raise holy Toledo with me for forgetting it. You bought it for me to take whenever I went walking alone. I didn't see any lights on in any of the cottages and I didn't want to terrify anybody by pounding on their door. I know, I could have come around the side of your cottage and rapped on the window and woken you up, but there's something about finding a dead body and knowing it was a gruesome murder that gets me deep down. It's not my first murder, it's not even the first one involving a knife—the last one in California was a young woman who was killed in almost exactly the same way. It's an ugly discovery, it's something about knowing you were too late to stop all the blood loss; no, I couldn't barge in. I needed to walk it off.

And even if I did wake some family up, after I used their phone to call 911 I'd have to wait around for the squad car to show up and then go back with them to the body and answer a hundred questions—and me barefoot! That would not look professional."

He put his arm around Teresa. "By then you'd have called out the National Guard to look for me. So I walked back to call the police from our apartment and work it through my brain and also get some shoes on."

"And then what happened?" I asked him. "Did they take the body away on a stretcher? Did they call the—is it the coroner? What do you call the guy who determines the cause of death?"

"Lizzie, where did you learn that language?" Digger asked.

"It's in the newspaper whenever there's been a mysterious death."

"I give up," he said. "You're right. It's called the medical examiner."

"Yes, the medical examiner. And did they dust the body for fingerprints? How about on the jetty, did you find any clues?"

"Lizzie's into reading detective stories," my mom said. She said it like she was apologizing for me, so I tried not to ask anything after that.

Digger went on to tell us that there was no identification on the body. "No wallet or keys, but maybe they'll find some labels in his sweatpants and sweatshirt. He was wearing a sort of ratty suit jacket and it had an L.L. Bean label but from the looks of him, he probably got it at a Goodwill store."

"You didn't find a single clue?" I couldn't help asking. I was disappointed.

"The one item that might provide a clue though, was a silver flask in one pocket."

"A silver flask just for water?"

Digger smiled. "No, *mi amor*, for liquor."

"But it'll probably have fingerprints on it, don't you think?"

"Possibly. But if the victim hasn't ever been arrested his fingerprints won't be on file."

"Maybe you can figure out where he bought it."

"Maybe, my little detective. I know one detail about the killer that may prove useful going forward."

"You do? What is it? Tell us, Digger."

"I'll tell you but I don't want this to be known outside this room until I discuss it with the police. As of now I have offered my services. Of course I presented my credentials from Montandino, California."

I said, "We promise, we promise. Now tell us."

"The murderer was left-handed."

"Is that all? How could you tell?"

"The murderer had to creep up on the victim from behind, just as I did. He had to use his left hand to cut the man's throat from right to left, do you follow me? If he were right-handed, he would have cut from the left side of the victim's throat."

Teresa tsk-tsked. "We've only been here six months and already you're involved in solving a homicide."

"Digger, I just thought of something."

"What, *chica*?"

"Jeb Blanco is left-handed."

Digger let out a low whistle. "This is a detail you must not mention to the reporters, you understand? I must tell it to the authorities first."

"I promise. Do you want me to raise my right hand?"

Digger smiled. "Lizzie, I trust you."

Well, you can just bet Digger's story got in the newspaper. Not just the local Woodvale paper, but the *Miami Clarion & Bugle* too. His picture was on the front page in both of them. And alongside the Digger we knew in sweatpants and baseball cap was a different Digger in a proper shiny chief of police hat and uniform with gold braid on the cuffs of the sleeves and upside-down *v*'s on the arms. Teresa told me the *v*'s were called hash marks and they stood for all the years he served as chief in their hometown in California.

The detail about which hand the murderer used was not in the papers. Digger said the police had agreed with him to withhold this information for the time being. They interviewed two local police officers also but they didn't add anything to what Digger had said. It was "The case is under investigation" and so forth, which Digger said was the usual.

When Digger gave a television interview for our local station, the reporter asked him how he felt about all the attention he was receiving. We saw his answer that evening on the six o'clock news.

"I'm used to it," Digger said. "It happened often enough in California. Even in a little town we had our share of excitement."

Teresa kind of snorted. "My modest husband."

I could hardly wait to get to my computer so I could email Trippy all the latest info. I was dying to tell her that Digger knew the murderer was left-handed but I had promised not to, so I just told her about how he found the body. Just imagine opening an email from your best friend and finding out that a man had been killed practically on top of where she lives.

CHAPTER 13

Well, the next day right after Mom drove me home from school, there was Digger dressed in his chief of police uniform again, waiting with two police officers in front of our cottage. In my whole life this has never happened to me before. For just a second I thought they had come to arrest me because I knew about Julio from the day Trippy and I discovered the warehouse and I hadn't told right away, and that the woman officer was there to strip-search me before they put me in a jail cell.

But it turned out they only wanted to interview me and Mom (which of course should be *Mom and me*), because we had both met Jesús Ernesto Blanco, who said to call him Jeb.

Mom invited them in and we all sat in a row in the living room as dumb as doorstops and then the male officer, who said to call him Officer Frank for Frank Franklin, began.

"Now Lizzie, your mother has described how you and she first met Mr. Blanco. Do you remember anything special about him?"

So I had to tell about the royal-blue shirt with some sort of monogram and the shoes with tassels. And the blue eyes and the rimless glasses that made him look like a professor.

And then I said that I thought I knew him from somewhere else, but when I said so he said he had the kind of face that everybody thought looked like somebody else. In Philadelphia he said a man stopped him on the street and was positive Jeb Blanco was his second cousin.

"You're very observant," Officer Frank said and I saw his lips were twitching with what I thought was a smile. He was scribbling away in his notebook. "I must ask you not to divulge this information to the press, do you understand what that means?"

Of course I knew the word *divulge*. It has a neat origin from the Latin *di-vulgare*, to spread among the people—that's where we get the word *vulgar* too, but I also knew I hadn't divulged anything.

I suddenly had a flashback to two men I saw on the jetty where one was fishing, or maybe just pretending to be fishing while he waited for his buddy, and the other one was picking his way out to visit him. I was watching through my binocs and I thought to myself that the visiting man looked familiar, and my heart started to pound. Could it be Jeb Blanco! But I was too flustered inside to say anything to Officer Frank. "You understand, Mr. Blanco is now a person of interest."

I waited for my heart to slow down and then I looked at Mom. I asked her, "Did you tell about what Henry said? About the plan to give away the land and all?"

"Yes, I reported the entire conversation."

"So why don't we move on?" the woman officer said. Her name was Officer Brianna Hermann Kasperowicz and it barely fit on her yellow metal name tag. I wondered if the tags were custom-made for each officer, or did they buy one size and have to squeeze the letters on. This is the kind of thing that happens to me all the time where words are concerned, when I should be paying attention to the question.

". . . after your mom went in the house with Henry," she was saying. "Tell us what you did next."

So I described Trippy wheeling my chair out past the vegetable garden, out through the cornfields, wheeling my chair between rows, one field after another, and how we finally came to the warehouse they all knew about from Digger. I corrected myself and said Chief Diego Martinez.

"But you didn't tell anyone what you saw when you peeked in," Officer Frank said rather crossly. "Specifically, not even your mother that day. Why not?"

"It's hard to explain. Trippy and I knew we were probably trespassing and then we met this kid who turned out to be Julio who seemed sort of scared and he made us promise to keep him and the monkeys a secret. So that made us think the whole thing was dangerous, and we were scared, so we agreed not to say anything when we got back to Henry's."

"But your own mother?"

"I wanted to tell Dig—Chief Martinez first."

"But even before you told Chief Martinez you told that other kid in a wheelchair from your school, named Joshua Blaine?"

That made me mad. "His being in a wheelchair had nothing to do with it any more than my being in a wheelchair did. The way you said it shows you have lumped us together as the two cripples." I knew I needed to cool it because you just don't say anything smart-alecky back to a policeman.

"Lizzie," my mom began.

But Officer Frank broke in. "Whoa, back off now. I wasn't lumping anybody with anybody else."

"Josh is my friend and I admit I told him first because he's the smartest person I know. It was his idea to Google Jesús Ernesto Blanco and find out what his background was. I swore Josh to secrecy, even under torture and in *durance vile*."

Officer Frank looked perplexed, but now my mom spoke up.

"Lizzie likes to use unusual phrases. In *durance vile* is from Middle English. It means under harsh confinement."

"Okay, and what did you find out about Blanco?"

So I told him everything we learned online, but I thought they must know all this by now, because they must have computers in the police station. He acted impatient and said, "Yes of course" while he went on scribbling, but I could tell that what I was telling him was brand-new news to him.

"But when you did tell Chief Martinez about the warehouse full of monkeys, what did he say?"

"He said we should go to the police."

"And why didn't you?"

"We were going to. But it was nine p.m. by then and I begged him to come with me the next day and see for himself. I thought telling what a kid saw might not be taken as seriously as what he saw. I figured we could go to the police right after that."

Officer Frank seemed to accept that explanation. He nodded.

"And then just as we drove up to the warehouse the door opened and this . . . this same kid who had told us his name was Julio came out. I didn't hear most of what they said to each other because I couldn't get out of the car but I knew Digger—I mean Chief Martinez—would find out who he was and what he was doing there and that way we'd have . . . a bigger picture to take to . . . to take to the authorities."

With that Officer Frank Franklin got up and said, "Thank you. You've been very helpful. Steps will be taken by the Florida Fish and Wildlife Conservation Commission to locate the tamarin monkeys. The interview is over."

"And what about Buddy and Blossom? The bear cubs?"

"They will be confiscated immediately and relocated to a conservation site."

So then I did a really stupid thing. I burst into tears. Not so much for the monkeys, although I know they are endangered and it was cruel and inhuman to capture them in the first place. I was crying for Buddy and Blossom. What would become of the cubs? And then Officer Brianna Longname came over and knelt down beside my chair. "I promise you that the cubs will go to an appropriate facility. Fish and Wildlife deal with this sort of problem every day and they are skilled caretakers."

I blubbered, "So I will never see them again."

"Maybe not," Brianna said. "But you'll know that you probably saved their lives. They might have been taken out and shot or they might have been taken somewhere and just let loose to forage for themselves."

"But they can't do that! They've had people caring for them from the time they were baby cubs!"

"Lizzie, I personally promise you the bears will go to a

good home. I will make it my business to track them and report back to you, okay?"

I nodded and tried for a smile.

"And as far as everything you told us goes, you did a great job. Josh may be the smartest person in the class, but I bet you're tied with him."

That made me feel a lot better. Afterward, Mom said she thought I bore up very well and that "shedding a few tears simply authenticated your testimony." It took me a little while to digest that.

Later that day a photographer from the Woodvale paper arrived to take our picture. I asked her, "How did you find out about us?"

She explained about the police blotter. "It isn't like a desk blotter for ink anymore, though I think that's where the word comes from."

I really liked her for being interested in words. "It's a record the police have to keep of every incident or crime in their jurisdiction. Because this is a democracy, every newspaper reporter has a right to read the blotter." So that's how she found Digger. And the next day Digger was on the front page again, splendid in his uniform, seen conferring with Officers Frank and Brianna. And Mom and I were on the back page opposite Josh and his mom Jenna and his brother Greg, who had just gotten back from his Latin class trip to Tuscany, in Italy, and Josh's father Will. And guess what? Josh's father turns out to be a doctor at Dirk Isle Hospital. Mom spoke to him about Henry's mother and he promised to look into it. And sure enough, we were in the *Miami Clarion & Bugle* too, but not on the front page. We were inside, on the bottom half of the second page. "Below the fold" is how they say it in the newspaper world.

I couldn't sleep that night from thinking about Jeb Blanco who had seemed so smooth and well dressed and who turned out to be the Villain with a capital *V* because he was *trafficking* in endangered animals. And it wasn't just the tamarins that were keeping me awake. I wondered if Jeb Blanco had something to do with the murder. Hadn't I seen him walk out on the jetty with his briefcase? Or was it just somebody who looked like him?

You can believe that Josh and I were suddenly everybody's best friend at Graver. Kids who snickered behind our backs in class or totally ignored us in the lunchroom now wanted to know if we could come over to their houses. Winnie Ellerman, who is the class beauty, offered me a makeup session at her house where she had an eyelash curler and eyeliner and blush-on and she could give me a manicure. "It would be lots of fun Lizzie, and I have the coolest CD collection, lots of stuff I bet you've never heard, like heavy metal."

I have to admit I was slightly tempted, especially about having my eyelashes curled. "I wish I could Winnie, but I think I have to come home every day after school to be available to the police."

"Are they going to indict you?" Herbie "Hotshot" Fayerweather asked. These were the first words he had ever spoken to me. "Because my father is a lawyer and I bet I can get him to take your case."

"But I haven't committed any crime! And besides I have a lawyer, he's my mom's boyfriend."

I couldn't believe I said that. But it was getting to be true.

CHAPTER 14

Well, we weren't done with interviews because the next morning before school Officer Frank arrived with another squad car marked MIAMI POLICE. *The gang of four*—that's what Mom called them afterward—knocked on the door. Actually, they knocked on the screen door because both the front and the back doors were open to air out the bacon smell from a little bit of overcooking I had performed.

Everybody trooped in and sat around the living room. Nobody wanted coffee. The situation looked dark.

Officer Frank spoke. "Lizzie, I want an honest answer. Did you tell Julio you had gone to the authorities? Is that why he left?"

I was astonished. "No! How could I? He has no phone. And I don't drive."

"We have information that your boyfriend's brother took you both in his car to an undisclosed location late yesterday."

I don't like to admit it but I have a temper. Mom says when I was a toddler I used to throw temper tantrums in the middle of an aisle at the supermarket, and I remember from those times how everything turned into a churning sea of red. That was what was happening right now. I took three deep breaths to calm the sea before I answered.

"First of all, he's not my boyfriend, we are merely"—here I stumbled over 'best,' then settled on 'good'—"friends. Second of all, Josh's brother Greg drove us in his own car to the farm stand out on 131 where you can buy Breyers ice-cream sugar cones, and he treated us both. I had chocolate-chip mint and I can prove it because I dripped some on my T-shirt and it hasn't gone through the wash yet in case you need the evidence."

There was some chuckling at this and then Officer Frank said, "Well, your monkey worker's gone missing and we were hoping you could provide us with a lead."

This was really hard. I didn't have any idea where Digger had taken him to be *placed in protective custody*, but I was pretty sure Digger didn't want anyone to know Julio had come back in the car with us. I wasn't going to volunteer anything more than a direct answer.

"I don't have a clue," I said. "I only know his name is Julio Blanco and his uncle Jeb—Jesús Ernesto Blanco—was holding him as a slave to take care of the tamarins and weed the garden and so on."

Then Officer Pedro Herrera from Miami Police spoke. "And to compound the situation, Señor Blanco has vanished."

"Vanished? But his plane is out in Henry's cow pasture."

"Not anymore. We seized it right after your last conversation with the Woodvale force."

"How do you seize a plane?"

He answered, "It has been impounded and flown to an airstrip under our control."

At that point Digger arrived a little out of breath. "¡*Hola*! I was taking my morning constitutional to the jetty and just as I turned around I noticed your squad cars out front."

I was so glad to see him I almost cried but I managed not to and settled down.

Nobody responded after he said *hola*, so Digger introduced himself to the officers he hadn't met yet. "Chief Diego Martinez, retired." After Officer Frank got up and shook his hand, the others got up like dogs in a dog-training class and shook hands all around, and Mom fetched a chair from the porch and we went on from there.

Digger said, "Julio Blanco is seventeen years old. He is, or was, a fugitive from justice. He was sent to the Big Mangrove detention facility only because there was no family member to release him to on probation. He is an orphan. His uncle was out of the country and could not be reached. After six months the boy ran away because he feared for his life."

"Feared for his life? From a staff member? I find that hard to believe."

"No, no. He was well treated there, he liked the work, which as you know has to do with saving the mangrove trees from encroachment."

"What was he afraid of?"

"Apparently he had served as a lookout in a home burglary. It was the classic kid crime—break in, grab what you can—but the homeowner reappeared before they were done, so they ran."

"Did he have a record?"

"No, he was clean. But he'd dropped out of school and was living on the street. The two perpetrators were caught by an alert traffic cop as they ducked past him."

"So then he agreed to identify the two perps?"

"Yes. They had prior arrests for break-ins, so they were going away. But other members of the gang are at large and he fears he has been fingered."

"So he was a gang member?"

"No. He wanted to join, and serving as lookout was to be his ticket in."

"Does this gang have a name?"

"They call themselves *Los Pícaros*. Ruffians, or rogues."

"Go on."

"By that time Señor Blanco had returned. Julio was the only child of his dead brother and sister-in-law, who were killed in a car crash a year earlier. He gave Julio a place to stay and enough money for groceries. In return he was to tend the gardens and fields and feed the birds—it seems that Blanco was dealing in exotic birds before the tamarins."

"What kinds of birds?"

"Tropical exotics. Parrots and macaws. Umbrella birds. He'd fly off with two or three at a time in boxes but Julio never knew the destinations."

There was a long silence while the officers digested this information. Then Digger continued. "Julio was clearly Blanco's prisoner. He had no transportation. Blanco told him several times that he was shielding him from the authorities at Big Mangrove, and more important, he was keeping him safe from *Los Pícaros*. He hinted that he could contact the gang at any moment, so Julio wasn't tempted to leave. Also by then he had developed a deep feeling for the little monkeys who were in his care alone. He installed big tree limbs for them to climb, and baskets to serve as sleeping nests. 'They became my family,' he told me."

"And what about Blanco, where is he from?"

"He is originally from Miami. Julio said he didn't know where he was living now, only that he came and went by plane. Once he had disposed of the tropical birds he went away for a long while."

"Did he know where he'd gone?"

"Julio couldn't be sure, but he thought Central or South America. When Blanco returned he had the tamarin monkeys and a stack of cages and Julio helped his two accomplices unload the plane and put the cages together. The monkeys had been transported in burlap bags and were badly dehydrated. Julio immediately supplied them with water."

Officer Frank turned aside to confer with the others. "We need to research these . . . What did you call them, tamar-minds?"

"Tamar-*ins*," Digger said. "Golden lion tamarins, they're rare and endangered. Efforts are being made to save them through captive breeding."

I was impressed. Digger had done some homework.

He went on. "Apparently the shack Julio was living in had once been a storage facility for citrus equipment. That is where he found the wicker baskets, so he went out and cut some gumbo-limbo tree limbs to put in the cages and then he tied the baskets up high for nests."

Then one of the Miami officers had a bright idea. "Did you discover any connection to drugs involving this fugitive?"

"I beg your pardon?" Digger drew himself up. "Of course if I had I would have reported it. Like you, I am an officer of the law."

They didn't ask Digger if he had any idea where Julio had gone. I had been holding my breath waiting to hear what he would say, but I was spared.

Right then the memory of those two men on the jetty came back. If only it hadn't been so dark, if only I'd been watching a little earlier. But I just kept quiet.

The reason I didn't speak up was I still wasn't positive the man was Blanco. After all, look at all the other times that people thought he was somebody else. Suppose I was wrong? Then I would have fingered the wrong man. *To finger*, a transitive verb meaning to inform on.

That concluded the interview. After the squad cars had driven off Mom made some coffee for Digger and herself and I had another glass of orange juice while we all calmed down.

Finally Mom drove me to school and explained why I was late. In English class I slipped a note to Josh. *Cops again. Looking for Julio.* At lunch we were once again the most popular kids in the class.

"You mean the cops came all the way from Miami to grill you?" Herbie asked. And Winnie Ellerman repeated her invitation to do a complete makeover of my face next Saturday. But I couldn't tell them anything.

I shook my head and said, "I'm not allowed to divulge any information."

Seeing Jeb Blanco on the jetty was weighing on my conscience. I didn't mention it when Officer Frank Franklin was grilling me because not being super sure—sort of not trusting my own eyes—kept holding me back. Still, why in the world hadn't I told Digger? When Mom came to collect me I asked if we could stop at Teresa and Digger's. Aurelia was there fussing over Teresa, who had a bad cold.

"Don't come in, don't come in! I'm full of germs!"

"I just need to talk to Digger, *abuelita*. I'm sorry about your cold. Can he come out?"

Digger materialized eating a raw carrot. "Is Teresa very sick?" I asked him.

"No, it's just a nasty cold. You know, the kind with a stuffy nose and runny eyes. Not dangerous but not fun."

"What are you eating?"

He waggled the carrot at me. "This is all I'm allowed between meals," he complained. "I've already eaten two. Want a bite?"

I nodded and he broke me off a piece from the unchewed-on end. But before I put it in my mouth I took a deep breath and said all in a rush, "Digger, I have something to tell you I didn't tell the Miami policeman, I don't know why. But you remember when he asked you if Julio had been involved with drugs and you said, 'Like you I am an officer of the law?'"

"I remember it well, *chica.*"

"Well, I think I saw Jeb Blanco or somebody who looks like Jeb Blanco again out on the jetty."

"When was this?"

"I think it was Monday night. I was sitting on the back porch with my binoculars looking at the last sandpipers before they went away for the night. I keep a little chart of how late they stay. They stay later in good weather than they do in the rain, but that's not the point—only that's how I came to see two men out on the jetty in the almost-dark. They were talking and waving their hands as if they were having an argument. I was playing with Tigger. You know how you trail her little toy mouse along the floor and she'll pounce on it and so on. The sandpipers had already gone. I got a glimpse of one of the men. I caught the glint of light off his glasses. I'm almost positive it was Jeb Blanco."

"*Ay, mi vida*, this is very big news."

"What will happen now? Will I get arrested because I didn't tell them earlier?"

"No, because it was a detail you only remembered on this day, *chica*, you understand?"

I nodded but it wasn't exactly true.

"I will take care of it, *chica*."

CHAPTER 15

he next day was Saturday and I spent most of it at Josh's. Mom had gone out with Aurelia and Teresa for the day, to look at wedding dresses. Aurelia and Tom the Lion were actually going to do it! Get married, and I would be invited to the wedding. So today I'd been invited to stay with the Blaines. Josh and I did our algebra homework first. Mr. Hammersmith or The Hammer, as he is known behind his back, always gives us some real brainteasers over the weekends. They're optional for extra credit. Like this one:

It is possible for a set to have no elements. For example, there are no horses 25 hands tall (a hand is 4 inches). Such a set is called a null set, expressed by a pair of empty brackets { }. List ten other examples of a null set.

Most of the kids groan but Josh and I both think they are fun to work on. We came up with about thirty examples, like the set of months that begin with the letter *K*. Or the set of odd numbers exactly divisible by 4. Monday, when kids turn in their answers, The Hammer will hold up the wrong ones and say things like "near-ums don't count," or "close but no cigar." He says it in a nice jokey way. You wouldn't think it to look at him in a suit and tie but he's really a very sweet person.

Then Josh wrote an essay on the Bill of Rights for his history class and after he was done I borrowed his laptop to write an essay on *The Scarlet Letter* for my English class. I asked Josh if he'd ever read it.

He said, "I think I did, but I don't remember it well."

So I described the plot. "The story seems so old-fashioned. I mean, I feel sorry for Hester, but even sorrier for little Pearl, who is probably going to grow up with a depressed mother. And anyway, I can think of a dozen women on TV who could be wearing the big *A* on their pinafores, if we still had pinafores."

We both laughed. And then I emailed the essay to myself so I could print it out at home on Mom's printer. With those chores out of the way, we got to talking about the murder on the jetty that Digger discovered and all the excitement it created. Josh said he thought the murder victim was probably in some gang that was out to get Jeb Blanco, who had once been a member too and Jeb Blanco killed him instead.

I said, "Maybe Jeb owed him money so he killed him."

"But how did he get out on the very tip of the jetty in the middle of the night?" Josh asked.

"Maybe he came by boat."

"In that case, where's the boat?"

Then I said, "Jeb Blanco is giving me the creeps. Can we play Scrabble instead?" Josh really trounced me. He built *m-o-s-q-u-i-t* into the end *o* of my *m-o-t-t-o* and he managed to block me out of two triple word score chances. Scrabble can get to be a very fierce game. Mom and I have stopped playing because I am very competitive and I can't stand to lose every time, but it's even worse if she *lets* me win. I don't know why I take it so hard. It's a mother-daughter thing. But when Josh won I didn't mind at all. Josh's mom Jenna had bought fresh bluefish for dinner, and corn on the cob, which we shucked on the back deck. That's one thing I can never get over in Florida. You can eat fresh corn like, forever. In Wisconsin it's an eight-week . . . *phenomenon,* and that's it.

Josh's dad Will and his brother Greg tended the fish on the outdoor grill with a lot of kidding and poking each other with the baster. They were supposed to be using it to baste the fish with this special sauce Jenna had made from limes and I don't know what. When it was ready we all assembled around the dining table and took turns rolling our ears of corn on the stick of butter that had been "sacrificed for the greater good," Jenna said. Dessert was strawberries to dip in melted chocolate. I couldn't help feeling how terrific it was to have a father there picking the bones out of his fish, and chewing his ear of corn keyboard-style all along one row and then the next, and even talking with his mouth full. Talking about Greg's soccer team's chances of going to the state championship, and about how sweet it was not to have to worry about the phone ringing to call him to the hospital because he wasn't on call tonight. Josh had said that his dad was gone every other weekend when he had to stay out at Dirk Isle, and so they mostly didn't see him from Friday till Monday night. We sat around the dining table just pleasantly chatting until the sun started to go down. Then Jenna said she would drive me home in the van, so Greg rolled me up the ramp and Jenna fastened me in and when we got to our cottage she unfastened me and let me shoot down the ramp the way Josh does. That was sweet too.

It turned out Mom wasn't home yet, but the back porch door was open, so Jenna helped me get in. "I'll wait around till she gets here," Jenna said.

"No, don't bother, I stay home alone lots of times when Mom isn't here."

"You're sure?"

"Positive. I'll be fine."

"Okay. But promise me you'll lock the door when I leave."

I thanked her again for a lovely time. And then I said, "You have a very nice family." My voice kind of squeaked as I said it. I didn't realize I was close to tears. Jenna said, "Thank you Lizzie" in a sort of surprised voice and then she bent over and gave me a hug. Then she went out the front door and I locked it behind her.

I wheeled around and turned on a few lights. Mom and the Scarecrow had gone out to dinner—she'd left a note to tell me where they were and also to say that her cell phone was on if I needed anything. I leaned back in my chair and daydreamed about how it would be with the Scarecrow as my father, cheering me on at the debate team finals or just grilling bluefish for a family dinner. Maybe we could find Julio and bring him to live with us and just as I was imagining adding a room to the back of our garage I heard footsteps in the kitchen.

"Mom?" I said, though I knew it wasn't Mom, and suddenly a hand came down hard across my face. It was a man's hand I knew. He tied a bandanna so tight over my mouth that I couldn't scream and then he tied my hands together with another one. Then he scooped me out of my chair while I kicked feebly and squirmed against his body, but it was no use.

He kicked the back screen door open with one foot, then he slipped around the side of the house and threw me into the back of a large car and we shot away from the curb. I was on the floor of the backseat, wriggling and moaning and he said, "It's no use *pequeñita*. Give it up." That's when I knew for sure it was Jeb Blanco. *Pequeñita*. That's what he always called me.

He didn't say where we were going, but I knew. Don't ask me how, but I felt it in my bones, so it was no surprise when we turned off smooth highway and bumped onto dirt and then turned again. He shut off his headlights as we crept forward and I knew we were on the little road that led to Julio's shack.

When he finally stopped the car he got out and pulled out a penlight—you know, one of those tiny flashlights you can shine around in a small circle to find something you've dropped in the dark. By craning my neck up I could just make out the shape of a big padlock and I figured the police had padlocked Julio's shack to preserve the evidence. They always put yellow tape around buildings or holes in the street to preserve evidence while they think about the next thing to do. Blanco cursed under his breath, but in Spanish so I didn't know what he was saying. He came back to the car and popped the trunk. Then he went back to the lock and I saw he had a hacksaw in his hand. Once he'd sawed the lock open he came around to the back door of the car to get me. I desperately wanted to fight him off but he was

right, it was no use. He hauled me out like a bagful of monkeys. Kicked the door open, walked in, and dumped me onto a bed. Even in the dark I knew it was Julio's bed.

But what he did next was really scary. He shoved the bed with me on it farther into the corner against the wall. Then he set the penlight down under the bed so it cast only a small circle of light on the floor. There was a ratty dusty rug that had been beside the bed and I watched while he rolled it up. To my horror I saw there was a narrow trap-door hidden underneath where the rug had been. He knelt down muttering and rooting around until his hands closed on the ring that let him pull it open. And then I was terrified because I knew he was going to put me down there. I moaned and shook my head back and forth but he just said in this calm voice, as though he had done this a hundred times before, "It's no use *pequeñita.* No use at all. You will wait here for Julio."

Then he went out of the shack and I figured he'd gone to look for a ladder and I was right, because about five minutes later he came back in dragging this big wooden ladder, like from before the Civil War. It was so old it was full of splinters, which he kept cursing at and stopping to suck a finger. It took him a long time to wrestle it into place. Then he went down it testing each step. I could hear him bouncing on them one at a time and then he came back up and came over to pick me up.

I struggled and fought as hard as I could until he said, "Listen, *niña*. Either we go down the ladder together or I just drop you down and forget about you, do you hear me?"

I nodded my head yes. Though which was better—to

die instantly from being dropped on my head or to die of starvation and dehydration in *durance vile*? Because Julio was never coming back here. He was in protective custody someplace safe. I hoped he was happy there.

Once Jeb Blanco got me down the ladder I huddled on the damp dirt floor and started sobbing. I couldn't help it. This was worse than my worst nightmare. He watched me for a couple of minutes and then he went back up the ladder and pulled the mattress off Julio's bed. He threw it down so that it landed right next to me and he said, "There. Pull yourself up on that. I know you can."

So I did. And then he threw me down this ratty old army blanket. "You will stay down there until Julio comes back, you understand?"

He didn't wait for an answer but went back up the ladder. I watched the trapdoor close over me, leaving me in the pitch dark. Then I heard him unroll the rug and pull the iron bedstead back over it and then I heard him dragging in something, most likely some old wooden boxes that had once held birdseed and bunches of bananas. I could hear him grunting as he worked, and from the thumping I gathered that he was stacking them on the bed. Then the outside door closed and after that I couldn't hear anything because I was sobbing so hard. I cried for about five minutes and then I got hold of myself and sort of snugged the blanket up around me as best I could with my hands tied together. I had two forever useless legs, and now my hands were all but useless too. I lay there thinking about how sorry for myself I'd been in the hospital after my accident. A kid just about my age tried to make friends with me there. He had been in a pickup truck rollover and his spinal cord was severed so his arms and legs were paralyzed and he was a quadriplegic. He lay on his back and spoke into a little tube that hung over his face. This was what he had to live with every day for the rest of his life. I wondered where he was now or if he was even still alive. In the total blackness I couldn't do anything except lie there with four fingers holding that musty old blanket. I wondered how long it would take me to die.

I thought about how it must have been when Mom came home all bright and cheery and called, "Lizzie?" and then she and the Scarecrow saw my empty wheelchair and no sign of me. Mom must have totally freaked out when she couldn't find me. I wondered what she did next. Did she sit down and cry or did she pick up the phone and call Digger and then the Woodvale police and then the Miami police? Or was she crying so hard that she couldn't talk and so she handed the phone to the Scarecrow and he made the calls? And then I thought about Digger and Teresa, who were my *abuelito* and *abuelita*, and I thought that Teresa would have come over to our cottage right away to hold and comfort my mother and that Digger was already figuring out that I had been kidnapped by Jeb Blanco. But where would Jeb Blanco have taken me? Had he dropped me off the jetty to drown? What would Digger do? I cried a lot more. Some of it was over Josh who I might never see again just as we were getting started on a real friendship, and then I cried because I wouldn't get to see Lia and Tom marry, and would the Scarecrow marry my mother after I was dead and on and on.

CHAPTER 16

*a*t some point I must have dozed off, because when I woke up I heard the sweetest sound in my life, which was men's voices and I knew they had come to rescue me. I tried to call out but of course I was gagged so the only sound that came out was a sort of gargle. I heard them exclaim over the broken padlock. Then there was the welcome sound of heavy boots entering the shack and their voices as they poked around in the wooden boxes and stomped into the corners. I couldn't make out the actual words, but I thought I recognized Officer Frank's voice. And then to my horror the voices moved away and the door closed and silence crashed back down on me like a grand piano dropped by mistake from a high-rise apartment.

I started to sob again. You would think that there couldn't be any tears left by now, but there were. My chest hurt from heaving up and down and my nose was so stuffed up that it was getting hard to breathe and I was scared I would suffocate before I could starve to death. Years and years from now when somebody found the trapdoor and opened it, there would just be this pile of bones with a disgusting snotty bandanna still attached to the skull.

I don't know how long I lay there thinking about how

much my mom would miss me and how Tigger would be all confused by my absence—and even The Hammer in Algebra I would notice I was gone, so then Josh would get to answer every problem the rest of them were stumped by. And Josh, the real Josh, how much would he miss me?

My thoughts were jumping around all over the place now, from the Scarecrow to Lia and Tom and to my honorary grandparents I had come to love, when I suddenly heard another sound. A car door slammed and footsteps came running up to the door, then entered. Then I heard the sound of wooden boxes crashing down and then I heard the iron bed getting pushed back against the wall and the rug ripped away. Fingers found the ring on the trapdoor and flung it open. Daylight shone in and made me blink. Then a head peered in, blocking the light.

"¡*Madre mía*! My poor baby! At last I've found you," said a familiar voice. And Digger started down the ladder. It took him only a minute to untie the bandanna from around my mouth and another minute to undo the one tying my hands together. Then he sat down beside me on that grotty mattress and folded me to his chest and rocked me back and forth as I blubbered some more. "Shh, *mi amor*, shh. It's over, it's over, it's all right now," he murmured.

"But how did you know where to find me?"

"Fifty years in police work, *toda mi vida*, fifty years of uncovering evidence and solving crimes, I knew where to look. I tried to reach Julio to take him with me but there was no answer so I just jumped in my car and drove out here alone. The minute I came in, when I saw the bed in the middle of the floor, I knew at once it was covering something. In so small a shack the bed would normally be against one wall, right?" I sort of hummed against his chest so he went on.

"And these old storage buildings, often they had a root cellar. A cool place to keep the fruit until it could be packed for shipping. But never mind all that. Now, let's get you out of here."

He tugged me to my feet and pulled me as far as the ladder. But there was no way I could climb it. Digger studied the situation. Then he said, "Put your arms around my neck, *chica*. We will go up the ladder together." And we did. I could hear Digger grunting and straining under the load of my ninety-pound body. At last we were above-ground. The little shack looked like heaven to me then, with four walls, on terra firma, as Teresa would say. We both sat on the bedstead for a minute resting and then a terrible thing happened. Digger bent forward groaning, wrapping his arms around his chest.

"What is it what is it?" I yelled. "Oh Digger, is it your heart?"

He nodded, rocking back and forth holding his chest, and then he finally stretched out flat and pillowed his head on my lap. I saw his cell phone strapped to his waist and with a lot of wiggling and straining forward I was able to unhook it. It was just like Mom's phone. I tried to stop shaking as I dialed 911.

My hands were clammy but my voice was strong as I told the operator how to find us.

"It's on the little dirt road just past the turn to Wilder-wood on County Road 232." The operator told me to stay on the line until help arrived. I did, but meanwhile I was thinking that I gave Digger his heart attack—first with moving the heavy boxes, then with having to climb down the ladder and then, worst of all, carrying me back up piggyback. If he died it would be my fault.

I told myself that this was a *macabre* thought—from *danse macabre*, dance of death. It goes all the way back to the plague, the black death of the Middle Ages. I probably shouldn't do this with words, especially at a moment like this, but it's the only way I know to keep from screaming and pounding on things. The operator was still on the line. He kept asking me if the individual was still conscious. I kept bending down to talk to Digger and each time he murmured, "Still here, *chica*," so that much was good. It felt like it was taking forever. And then at last I heard sirens. Their wail grew stronger, and behind them I could hear the special bleating horn of an ambulance.

Everything happened so fast after that. It was crazy, like a series of flash camera shots popping one after another. Digger on a stretcher with medics on either side. Police from Woodvale and others from the towns around Wilderwood swarming through the doorway and filling up Julio's pitiful little shack. Some of them climbing down the ladder into the cellar—the trapdoor was still open—to look around. And then more medics kneeling beside me telling me I would have to go to the hospital in an ambulance too, just to be checked out after my ordeal. I kept saying I was fine, I just wanted to go home, but they said it was *protocol*. I haven't had a chance to look that one up but anyway, I knew it meant that whatever they said I would have to do it. And then Brianna Longname was there kneeling down to talk to me over all the hubbub, and she said, "Your mom and grandmother have gotten the news. They will meet you at the hospital. In fact they'll probably get there pretty soon after you do."

By then Digger had been carried out on his stretcher and two very nice medics loaded me into the back of the second ambulance. When I started to cry again and said it was too scary to lie down and be strapped flat after being tied up, they said I didn't have to, so they let me sit up and I had a medic on either side of me. One kept taking my blood pressure, which was also protocol and she said it was normal. The other kept giving me little paper cups of bottled water because I was so parched from being gagged. We had a police escort with siren and the ambulance driver used his horn every few minutes. I only wish I could have divided myself in two and one of me could have been in the other ambulance with Digger.

I had to wait for them to bring out a wheelchair to wheel me into the ER and then they took me into a cubicle with just curtains, no walls or doors, and helped me take off my grotty clothes, which was definitely okay with me. I never wanted to see those shorts and T-shirt again. A nurse helped me put on a johnny that tied behind my back. After that I had to lie on a bed there and just wait. I could see shapes of nurses and doctors going by outside the curtain and caught snatches of conversation, a lot of it about who was meeting who for lunch in the cafeteria. I worried and worried about Digger, who could be alive or dead, and maybe he was dead this minute and they weren't telling me, and then a hand reached up and swished the curtain open and a voice said, "Lizzie?" It was Josh's dad, Dr. William Blaine.

"I know you're worried about Chief Martinez, so let me tell you first that yes, he did have another heart attack, but it was a small one. He was lucky you were able to call 911 right away and we were able to medicate him promptly. We'll keep him here under observation for a few days and then he should be good to go, as we say."

"Can I see him?"

"Sure, just as soon as I check you out."

He listened to my heart, and then to my lungs while I took deep breaths and then looked in my mouth and down my throat and felt around behind my ears and down my neck. He looked at the scrapes on my legs from being hauled around and said they weren't serious—what he recommended was a long hot soak in bubble bath. *Exotically scented bubble bath* is what he actually said, which just proves that people are full of surprises.

Then my mom was there hugging me and crying, and then I cried too, and Dr. Will said, "I'll just fill out the necessary paperwork for discharge and leave you two to finish up." He said it in a nice sympathetic tone, as if it was okay to cry together, whereas he could have been sarcastic, which made me like him even better.

I had to put the same dirty clothes back on because Mom was too rattled to think to bring me clean ones when she heard where I had been found, but that was okay. They let us go up to the ICU and just peek in at Digger. Teresa was sitting in a chair on the far side of the bed and Digger was hooked up to a whole bunch of buzzing monitors that I suddenly remembered from after my accident. But he lifted his free hand and blew me a kiss. Teresa came out in the hall to speak to us. Mom said how sorry she was and I said how scared I was that I had caused it. Teresa said that although it was terrible that Digger had a second heart attack, "Think how good it was that it happened while Lizzie was there with him and she called for help right away."

"But Teresa, I think it was all my fault from his lifting those boxes and coming down the ladder and then carrying me up it piggyback."

Teresa shook her head. "It was bound to happen sooner or later. We knew his arteries were clogged to begin with, and he kept sneaking jelly doughnuts and apple pie from the 7-Eleven. The cardiologist is going to do an angioplasty and we're hoping he can put in two stents where the blockage is worst."

Angioplasty. Stents! My head was spinning from this new language.

CHAPTER 17

Well, in spite of everything that happened to me I didn't get to miss a single day of school because the *abduction*—from *ab*, away, and *dutere* to lead—a much better word than *kidnapping*—took place on a Saturday night. I can't believe I was home in my own house by noon on Sunday. Mom wanted me to take it easy the rest of the day so I propped myself up in bed and opened *Pride and Prejudice* again, thinking it would put me to sleep. It did. When I woke up the sun was going down and Jane Austen was lying on the floor open to chapter ten where Elizabeth refuses to dance with Darcy.

I won't even list the reporters for newspapers and TV stations who showed up that afternoon. Mom had a hard time getting rid of them, but she did sort of organize them so I wouldn't have to tell the story over and over. I didn't pose for a single picture but a swarm of photographers got me anyway. Brianna came to help control what she called the *paparazzi,* who are those sneaky photographers who hang around movie stars like pigeons, always moving just far enough away so you can't catch them. But the story of my abduction and rescue wasn't just local, it was national news! It made my flesh creep to see the replay of Mom and me being interviewed on every channel. And then a thousand pictures of Julio's shack, but they couldn't get inside it to snap the trapdoor because there was a cop there around the clock. You can be sure that if they could have opened it up to see the root cellar, they would have. Well, you can imagine, the emails back and forth with Trippy just flying through outer space. Now I had a *real-life drama* to tell her about. That's how they say it on TV. She had already read about the abduction on the *Clarion & Bugle*'s web page. I told her it was weird being famous all of a sudden. I didn't think I liked it much.

"You poor goonie!!! I would have died down there in that root cellar!!! But the famous part ought to be fun. I wish I could be down there with you and your mom and all."

I promised to keep her up-to-date every day from now on. Trippy was lobbying for another trip to Florida for her graduation from eighth grade. Her mother said the weather was awful in Florida in the summer and no one in their right mind would want to go there but if that was what she wanted. . . . Did Lizzie think her mother would let her come again?

"Of course she is welcome," Mom said. "It's important to hold on to old friends."

And speaking of old friends, a big surprise came in the snail mail. A letter from Tony! His dad had come home from the broadcast studio in Madison with the news right off the wire from the AP. That stands for the Associated Press. Tony said the story of my abduction was sick, really sick. He said it was boss, a hundred times bigger than the little kid stuff we had done like tying our sleds to his dad's car bumper, bigger than trying to sniff homemade snuff. It

made him feel way boss to be my old friend. And he hadn't forgotten those two candy bars. He wrote to me snail mail, just addressed to Woodvale, FL, with its zip code, because he didn't have my email but here was his. I emailed him a quick note saying more to come.

This was what being famous felt like and except for hearing from Tony, I hated it. The whole next week I cringed every time some kid at school would tell me she read the whole story in the *South Florida Gazette* or something. I just wanted to be normal again, or as normal as an eleven-and-a-half-year-old girl in a wheelchair who is graduating from eighth grade in couple of months can be.

Josh was the only one who didn't badger me with questions. In fact he didn't ask a single one. But I asked him to ask his dad when Digger would get out of the hospital and he wheeled up to me the next day and said, "Good news."

We were just on our way to the cafeteria for lunch. "The angioplasty was a piece of cake according to the cardio." (That's med-speak for cardiologist.) "They put in two stents—you know, those little mesh things that hold the arteries open—and got him up that afternoon. He only has to stay overnight and then they'll discharge him."

"So then he won't just have another heart attack?"

"Nope. He should be good to go, but he has to show up three times a week for six weeks for cardio rehab."

"What's that?"

"It's like a class for people who've had heart attacks and are now recovered but they have to work out on exercise bikes to get their heart rate up and learn how to eat right and stuff like that."

"Poor Digger! No more jelly doughnuts."

"No, but he got his life back."

Speaking of hearts, mine was just about broken by Josh's big news. He's been accepted by Phillips Andover Academy, which is a fancy prep school way up in Massachusetts. Josh claims it isn't fancy at all and that they have a very *diverse* student body which Graver doesn't have—though we do have two Indians from India in our school and one of them, Vijay in the class below us, is so smart it's scary. "If you do well at a prep school like Andover your chances of getting into a really first-rate college are very good," Josh said.

"Because you want to be a doctor, like your dad?"

"Well, that's a long way off. But when I get there I want to specialize in CP and other things like it. You can specialize in neurology and study what shuts down in the brain and try to figure out why."

I didn't say anything but I was thinking how much I'd miss him.

"But we have the whole summer to hang out," he said as we rolled through the cafeteria line, choosing chicken fingers and chili.

"I'm going to stay at Graver right through high school because I need to stay in a warm climate."

Josh found the right thing to say. "There're lots of top-notch colleges in the South."

"Trippy is coming down for two weeks and right after we graduate. Mom is going to drive us all the way to the Georgia primate refuge where the tamarins are. She said we could spend a day there to watch how they're being rehabilitated. I wish you could come, Josh."

"I bet I could talk Mom into it." He reached his plate out for a chicken finger. "You want one of these? They're full of trans fat."

"Oh, sweet. I mean about coming to Georgia. And yuck, no. I'll take the chili."

"And what about the bear cubs? Do you know what happened to them?" I hadn't thought about Buddy and Blossom since the abduction what with everything else that was going on.

"Brianna is coming over for supper tonight and I'm sure she'll have some news."

CHAPTER 18

rianna, who says she is half German and half Polish, was at our stove making something she rolled up in cabbage leaves for supper. Tonight, she said, was her treat. I was sure I would hate it because just thinking about cabbage makes me want to throw up. You notice I didn't say puke because Mom says it is an offensive term. And barf is no better. But actually the *gefüllter krautkopf*—that's what Brianna calls it and I got her to write it down for me—was pretty good. It had hamburger and onions and a lot of chopped-up tomatoes in it so you could hardly taste the cabbage. I love the sound of *krautkopf*, though. It's German for cabbagehead and Brianna says it's an insult if you call somebody that. I figured it might come in handy.

Then I asked Brianna about Buddy and Blossom. We hadn't talked about them for so long that I was afraid they had been taken away and "disposed of," the way the police disposed of the dead body. After all, they couldn't just leave it around to rot. Digger said it was in a morgue, which is like a big walk-in freezer, until someone could identify it. Maybe that was what had happened to the cubs.

But Brianna said that the authorities had decided the cubs were too dependent on human contact to be good choices for getting reintroduced into the wild. "So," Brianna said, "they're going to this zoo in Virginia. It isn't a zoo with cages. The bears live in an artificial forest with a moat dug around to keep them in."

Mom said, "Well, that sounds like a good compromise. Because you know they could have starved to death out alone in the woods. They probably couldn't have fought off other bears for food. They've never hibernated, so they might not have known what to do in a northern winter."

I had to agree. Still, I felt very sad the rest of the evening.

But the next morning Digger came bursting in, full of good cheer. I was just beginning on my usual cornflakes and banana slices, so I asked him had he had any breakfast.

"No, *mi amor*, not yet but yes, I will join you."

Then Mom appeared. She had already put on the coffee. Digger pulled up a chair and accepted a mug full. "No, no cream thank you. And no sugar. I am a new man. But I will help myself to a little of Lizzie's milk, yes?"

And then he started telling us that he had interviewed Julio last evening and the things Julio had told him would make your hair stand up on end.

"But where is he?" I asked. "You said he was in protective custody."

"He is staying with Alton Hammersmith," Digger said firmly.

"Mr. Hammersmith? The Hammer? Our algebra teacher?"

"That is correct. 'The Hammer,' as you call him, is a friend of mine from our Thursday night poker game. When I asked him if he could accommodate a houseguest for a while, he said he'd be happy to."

"I didn't know you played poker!"

Digger went on. "Julio saw us all on television and he knew at once who the murdered man was."

Mom said, "Does this mean he will testify?

"He will. But first we must settle the probation issue. I will ask that he be permitted to stay with Alton and his wife Martha until his eighteenth birthday. He will be state's witness and even though there are no charges against him, I think it would be useful to have a good lawyer by his side."

The Scarecrow! I thought.

"My friend Rob," Mom said. "This is exactly his kind of case." And she took out her cell phone and pressed a number.

I thought, Wow! He's at the top of her list.

Mom took the phone into the other room. In a couple of minutes she came back with it and handed it to Digger. "I think you two better work out a plan."

Digger said, "I hate these little bitty things, that's why I never use mine. Where do I put my mouth?"

And Mom said, "Just speak normally. He'll hear you."

So it was a wrap, as they say on TV. The Scarecrow would drive up from Miami to Woodvale tonight and he and Digger would accompany their charge to the police station together.

"Where is the Scarecrow going to stay?" I asked.

"Right here," Mom said. "And that's enough conversation out of you, young lady. Hurry up or you're going to be late to school."

CHAPTER 19

*T*he next day Digger said I could come with him after school to see Julio. "I want you to hear what he has to say about the time he spent as his uncle's slave to see if there is any information you can corroborate."

Mom came too. We had to wait about half an hour for Mr. Hammersmith because he never left Graver until the last student had departed. That was *protocol*, a word I understood even better now.

This gave us time to play with some of the foster dogs Alton Hammersmith and his wife Martha were caring for. Mr. Hammersmith is tall and thin. Mrs. Hammersmith is short and plump with a face so perfect it reminded me of my special doll from when I was a child. She explained that they always had four dogs at a time, dogs that were sent to them by the SPCA to care for and socialize so they could be adopted. You can imagine that my view of The Hammer was changing.

One of the dogs was all white with a big bushy tail. She was very friendly and rolled over on her back to have her stomach scratched. Another was big and gawky and very sweet. One little mutt looked like she had been put together from other animals. She had an anteater nose and bat ears and she begged to come sit in my lap. The fourth one went and hid under the table as soon as we came in. I thought maybe it was my wheelchair that freaked him out but Mrs. Hammersmith said no.

"He's still very fearful. He was a street dog and had to survive eating scraps out of people's garbage until the volunteers caught him. Then he had to be neutered and have all his shots. So it's going to take a while for him to accept us."

She said this very cheerfully, as if this had happened lots of times and the dogs all got over their fears and turned into the kind you would want to take home.

Which of course I did. But Mom said firmly that we were not yet ready for a dog. Even Digger, who said he was not much of a dog person, said he thought maybe he and Teresa should begin to consider taking in a needy one.

Julio was different from the sort of withdrawn guy he had been when Digger and I found him at the warehouse. He said hello and smiled and soon he was lying on the floor letting two dogs lick his face at once. I could hardly take it all in. First The Hammer turns out to be a dog lover and next the fearful Julio, who made us promise we'd never seen him before the day Trippy and I first met him, turns into a . . . a normal. I sort of realized how scared he must have been on our drive back to Woodvale, not knowing where Digger was taking him, not knowing if this protective custody arrangement was for real or if it was a setup and the gang would find him there. He was so relaxed and happy that it was hard to put together this Julio with the one we'd met before.

Back then, he mostly spoke only Spanish. In fact, he

didn't speak English at all during the whole year he was Jeb Blanco's slave—Blanco and his accomplices only spoke Spanish to him. But The Hammer and his wife didn't speak a word of Spanish, so living with them was life being in a permanent English class.

Mrs. Hammersmith said, "Julio's been an enormous help with the dogs. He's taken over the feeding and much of the walking. He's ready for more as soon as this batch is ready to go."

"Isn't it hard, letting them go when you've gotten . . . like really attached to them?"

"Yes, in a way it is. But we know they're going to good permanent homes. And there are so many others that need foster care. Not just in Florida, all across the country."

"It's worse here in the South," Julio said. "People don't spay and neuter their dogs, so they breed more and more and they end up roaming in a pack on the street." I thought of Henry drowning his cat's kittens until we took her to be spayed. And how Julio had lived on the street too.

Just then, Mr. Hammersmith arrived. After he kissed Martha and tousled a couple of the dogs, he said, "I think we need some refreshments."

You would think the wife would disappear into the kitchen and come back with milk and cookies, but oh no. The Hammer himself did the honors and it was kumquats and oatmeal cookies he had baked from a special recipe.

"Alton loves to cook," Martha explained. "He likes to concoct his own recipes, he says it's like inventing new algebra problems."

Concoct, I thought to myself. And *kumquats*, my favorite

citrus, a sweet and sour mouthful. They almost rhymed.

"They're just about out of season," The Hammer said. "But I have an inside source."

It was time to hear Julio's story but first, Digger warned us. "This goes no further than here in this room."

Mom said, "Of course," as if it were the most natural thing in the world.

Julio said, "I saw the murdered man up close only once. I was in the warehouse cleaning the monkeys' cages and giving them a few banana treats and some fresh water after their evening meal when I heard the sound of a car arriving."

Digger prompted him. "Was your uncle there at that time?"

"Yes, because he had just come to bring me my groceries for the week. I heard him swearing, telling this other man who had just driven up that he had no right to come out here, and the other man cursed him back with words I won't repeat, but I was scared they would start to fight. Or pull a knife or a gun."

"So what did you do?"

"I crept out very quietly through the warehouse door and flattened myself against the wall where I couldn't be seen but where I had a clear view of the quarrel. If there was going to be a big fight I thought somebody might get killed. I didn't know what I would do then. I was too scared to try to come between them." There was a pause while Julio struggled with his feelings. His voice had cracked on *scared* and I was scared with him.

"Take your time, son," Digger said. "Just try to remember what you saw."

"He stood facing me for what seemed like hours," Julio

said. "I thought, This is it. This is when someone gets killed. So I tell you I would know his face anywhere. They were quarreling about money. The man facing me was furious that Jeb Blanco was cheating him out of his fair share and if Blanco didn't agree to a fifty/fifty split he—Carlos is what my uncle called him—said he would rat on him."

"Rat on him?" I asked, and Digger answered, "Tell the authorities. That's how you say it."

"Finally, my uncle's voice changed. You know how polite and smooth he can be in public? When you first meet him you think, Oh what a nice gentleman? Well, that's what he did. He grew soft and pleasant and said, 'Okay. You are right, Carlos, we are equal partners. But I don't have the cash here. If you will wait out on the end of the jetty tomorrow night after all the fishing people have gone, I will send a cigarette boat to you with $100,000 in $100 bills and you can count them on the spot.'"

"Is that a little speedboat? There are always lots of them whizzing around out there."

Digger said, "Yes," and nodded to Julio to continue.

"Carlos agreed. Then Jeb Blanco said, 'The little boat may be very late, maybe after midnight. It will have to come after the cruise ships have departed because the tender that brings the pilot back in also brings in the week's money. All of that takes time. You might have to take a little nap out there while you wait.'

"Carlos said, 'That's no problem. I have just the thing for a nap,' and then I saw him pat his pocket. He took out a silver flask and showed it to Blanco. Then they each took a sip to seal the agreement."

I got very excited. "The flask! Remember Digger, when you searched the body and you found a silver flask? And we both said it could be a clue?"

"I remember, *chica*."

Then Digger added, "You did a good job retelling. Now comes the unpleasant end of the story. You must come with me and the officers to identify the corpse."

I said, "All this time Carlos's corpse, blue with cold, has been lying on a slab in the morgue in the dark with a ticket tied to his toe labeled UNKNOWN."

Mom said, "You've been watching too many detective stories on TV, Lizzie."

Which was true but wasn't this a detective story? And hadn't Julio come forth to solve it? Even if it meant he would be put back in juvie and the gang might get him?

When we said goodbye and thank you to the Hammersmiths, Martha Hammersmith said, "Come see us again anytime Lizzie. It's good for the dogs to experience new people and new situations."

I thought the "situations" had to do with my wheelchair, but I just smiled and thanked them both again for the refreshments.

"Bye Lizzie. See you around," Julio said. "Anytime you'd like to help me walk the dogs . . . I could push your chair."

I knew that was hard for him to say. "It's a deal. If you push I can hold a leash in each hand."

CHAPTER 20

The rest of the school year went by in a flash. All of a sudden it was time for Josh and me to graduate from eight grade.

Teresa wanted to throw a big party for us.

"No, *abuelita*, please don't fuss." I tried to explain that it isn't exactly a major event to graduate from middle school.

But of course she and Digger came to the ceremony in the school auditorium. The place was crammed. They sat in the front row. Mom and Josh's whole family sat right behind them and just as the disc playing the graduation song began, Dr. Will's cell phone started to vibrate. He whispered something to Jenna and went out, down the side aisle.

I knew we would have to cross the stage in alphabetical order, so that meant Josh would be second, behind Eloise Armansky. He scooted out in his electric chair and took his diploma gracefully from the president of the George W. Graver Academy, Ms. Hermina Rodriguez, who we almost never saw. When you're the president of a private school grades K through 12, you're on the road most of the time fund-raising but you make sure you get back in time for graduation. I know this because that was the way it worked at my mom's private college in Wisconsin. Anyway,

I was number 14 in line and I aimed my chair straight at the president. I stopped in exactly the correct spot, took my diploma with one hand and shook her hand with the other. She said, "Congratulations Lizzie, I am proud of you," and I said, "Thank you," and poof! I was a high school freshman. Freshwoman. Freshperson. I was in the first year of high school.

When it came to placement in the class, Josh and I cleaned up. He was first and I was second. Mr. Hammersmith said, "It could have been the other way around, that's how close you were." I knew he wouldn't say so just to make me feel better. I know the grade for my final essay in English class could have been improved *with the judicious use of commas*, but if you've gotten this far, you've seen all the commas I've put in to make up for it. I feel I have paid the comma price.

I got an A+ in Latin at least, and a little plaque in the shape of a shell. It says AD ASTRA! which means *to the stars* as if this was Hollywood. Josh won the math prize, a little bust of Archimedes, the father of mathematics. It looked to me like one of those busts of Beethoven kids get at the end of the year from their piano teacher.

Well, we ended up having a party after all. While we were busy graduating, Aurelia and Tom had secretly organized a big spread out on our porch, with Tom cooking hot dogs and hamburgers on a grill they had set up out on the beach, and Lia handing 'round potato chips and pretzels and pouring quarts of lemonade—the real kind, with fresh lemon slices. There was a surprise chocolate cake with CON-GRADULATIONS, GRADUATES written on the top in white icing. I couldn't tell if the *d* in *Congradulations* was there on purpose or because the cake icer couldn't spell. The Hammersmiths arrived with Julio and the Blaines all came. Dr. Will had returned from his emergency, Josh's brother Greg had brought along his girlfriend who didn't do sports but played a cool guitar.

I was sorry that Trippy had to miss the fun. She didn't graduate for another two weeks, but when she did, it was goodbye and curtains to Mercer Middle School and hello in September to North Side High. It would be scary starting over at the bottom of the ladder as a high school freshman in a three-story brick building with Up and Down staircases and an attached gymnasium. But in a way I envied her. She would be a minnow in the ocean of secondary school and I would be a big frog in the small pond that was Graver. In fact, my homeroom would be right next to The Hammer's math classroom and my second-year Latin class would meet in the same room I'd been wheeling to all year.

I haven't said so yet, but I liked my Latin teacher a lot. I liked the way she handled the four boys who always sat in the back of the room and cracked their gum and whispered to each other. She would say, "Will Sleepy Hollow please come to order?" and for some strange reason they did. Also she made many references to The Good Book, as in, "As The Good Book says, time and tide wait for no man." That had a cool mysterious sound to it. I am embarrassed to admit that it took me a whole year to figure out that The Good Book was the Bible.

Trippy, though, would get the chance to start over, getting to mix with kids from three other middle schools and make a whole bunch of new friends. Even a boyfriend. But in a way it was comforting to know I didn't have to make a big adjustment. I wasn't going to think about Josh's adjustment right now. The evening turned into a song fest, with The Hammer harmonizing with Tom and the Scarecrow in "Michael Row Your Boat Ashore" and "Kumbaya" and all of us chiming in as best we could. Who ever heard of an algebra teacher who rescued dogs and could sing baritone too? The evening ended in a kind of long drawn-out goofy version of "Good Night, Ladies."

CHAPTER 21

*R*ob the Scarecrow had news for us the next day. He had agreed to take Julio's case *pro bono*, which is short for *pro bono publico*, which means doing it for free for the good of the public. "But as it turns out, there is no case. Yes, he is on probation at the moment but it looks like Julio will be a free and independent citizen very soon."

"Is this because Jeb Blanco was holding him prisoner? Even though he paid for his groceries, is it still involuntary servitude?"

"Well, that would be a good reason Lizzie. But that's not why. He will be on his own the minute he turns eighteen. Then he will no longer be a minor and he will not need the Hammersmiths *in loco parentis*. There are no outstanding charges against him for the robbery because it was a first offense and no assault took place, so he can come and go as he wishes as of his eighteenth birthday."

"That's only a month away!"

"Right. It appears that his birthday is Bastille Day, July 14th."

Mom said, "How appropriate."

"Bastille, that was a prison in Paris, right?"

"Right. It's the day the people stormed the Bastille, the fortress where all the political prisoners were kept."

I could see why Mom said *appropriate*.

"Julio is essential to the prosecution of the case," Digger said. "Because he is the only person besides Jeb Blanco himself who knows who the victim is. Was. Even though he only saw him that one time, Julio is positive he recognized the victim."

"Wasn't he scared of seeing a dead body?" I asked Rob.

"On the way over I asked him how he felt about going to the morgue. He said, 'No, I've seen dead bodies before.' I didn't ask him where. Some things are none of my business."

I would have asked him where, I thought to myself.

And then Digger said to Rob, "Well, it won't be a piece of cake. You know how unreliable eyewitness testimony is. And we still don't know who Carlos is or what part he played in this business."

"And now he can't tell us," I said.

Rob agreed. "It won't be easy to have Julio's identification accepted without any corroboration. But I think we can make it stick."

Corroboration. Digger used it earlier, so it was time to look it up. Well, who would guess that the root goes all the way back in Latin to *robur,* literally oak. To make strong as oak.

By the time Trippy arrived it was really summer. Hot. Humid. Showers followed by rainbows. Too hot to hang out on the beach but we did go swimming every day even when there was lots of grungy seaweed to squish through. She described her graduation with the high school orchestra playing "Pomp and Circumstance" as the class came forward one by one for their diplomas. How two of the boys had upended a bottle of cherry brandy filched from one of their houses just before the ceremony started and they staggered so badly lining up that they had to be escorted from the premises. Trippy's mother said it was a scandal but her father said, "Boys will be boys."

"Did they get to graduate? Or were they expelled?"

"No. I mean, they didn't get to graduate with the rest of us or go to the class party after but they're going to North Side High in the fall. I know this because one of the mothers belongs to the same book club as my mother. That boy's mother says entirely too much is made of finishing middle school and transitioning to high school. There is absolutely no need for a graduation ceremony."

"Especially if your kid gets drunk for it."

One afternoon Mom drove us over to visit the Hammersmiths and let Trippy meet the dogs. The big white friendly dog with the bushy tail was gone.

"She got adopted into a terrific new home," Julio said. "Three kids and a big backyard with a fence. They've had dogs before, their last one also came from a shelter and lived to be sixteen. So they were sad, but ready."

"Is sixteen old?"

"Very old for a big dog. Little dogs live longer. Come see who took her place."

A big ribby sort of part greyhound and part collie stood quivering by the kitchen door. "It's all right Sasha, we can all go out—" And then Julio realized there were three steps from the back door down to the ground.

Trippy was quick to act. "You get in front and catch the chair on each step and I'll bump it down one at a time."

"Good job, goonie," I told her. Once Julio turned to her, Sasha raced to the fence waiting for the rubber ball he threw. She leaped in the air and caught it cleanly, then raced back to the steps.

"She hasn't learned how to bring it to me and drop it yet. But for a dog that was found locked in a cellar and starved almost to death, she's doing well."

I remembered the root cellar and shuddered. Then I remembered Julio waiting for his uncle to bring him food, never knowing when he might come or when he might turn him over to the gang.

We played with the dogs all afternoon. The shy one who hid under the table during our last visit seemed to be one of the gang now. Julio was kept busy throwing balls and Frisbees and playing chase. When it was time to go he wheeled me around the side of the house to the walkway.

"Julio's really cool, isn't he?" Trippy said once we got into Mom's car and headed home. "He's so much fun to hang with. Remember how scared he was talking to us that first time?"

Mom said, "People change. When you give them a chance they can change." I thought of that first scared dog at the Hammersmiths who is now such a happy camper but I didn't say anything. *Julio, Julio*, I hummed to myself. I wouldn't be surprised if Trippy had been humming the same thing.

Well, we just had a few more days before Trippy had to fly back to Wisconsin and it rained almost every day. We spent a lot of time on the computer. We read everything we could find about sanctuaries for primates. We Googled Old

Harmony Refuge for New World Primates in Georgia and I decided then and there to save half of my allowance from now on to contribute to their fund.

For Julio's birthday Mom and Martha Hammersmith took him shopping for some new clothes. They had to practically drag him to the mall but he ended up with two new T-shirts, sweatpants, a hoodie, and new sneakers. We had ice cream and a cake with nothing written on it. Just before she brought it to the table, Mom lit nine candles—"Each one stands for two years because the cake will fall apart if I put any more on it"—and we sang "Happy Birthday." Julio got up and walked away from the table and for a second I thought we had hurt his feelings. But then I realized he was feeling cared for and it was hard to handle after all that time in the Bastille.

It took almost another month to catch Jesús Ernesto Blanco. Even though there was an APB on him, he had melted into the general Miami population and there was no sign of him. APB stands for all points bulletin, which is information that goes out to all points where a criminal might try to get away, like airports and the ticket counters of train and bus stations and to state troopers who patrol highways. Miami is a big city and a lot of people come and go in it all year round. Snowbirds start coming in November to get away from the cold. They start leaving in March to get home in time for the daffodils. A lot of families come over spring break to walk on the beach and swim and salesmen and CEOs fly back and forth all year. All it took to catch Jeb Blanco was a smart guard checking everybody's papers. He saw something fishy about the passport, I don't know how he knew it was phony but he quietly signaled to a policeman standing nearby and Blanco was captured.

"'The suspect was *apprehended* standing in line at the Miami airport, holding a ticket to Cat Island in the Bahamas. Blanco, his head shaved and sporting a trim goatee, was wearing mirrored aviators. He was carrying a false passport in the name of Ricardo Jimenez, a deceased fisherman, and offered no resistance. He has retained Fletcher Rockingham to represent him. Rockingham is famous for representing several notorious criminals in the past decade, chief among them the triple-murderer Rabbit Dykeman from South Carolina, who walked away on a *technicality*. Dykeman then flew to San Francisco and one week later committed suicide by jumping from the Golden Gate Bridge. His motive was never made clear, but it is *conjectured* that he was overcome with remorse.'" I was reading this aloud to Mom and Brianna and Rob from the *Miami Clarion & Bugle*. *Technicality* was easy but I had a little trouble with *conjectured*. It comes straight from the Latin. *Con* means together, and *jicere/jacere* means to throw, and some of the things thrown together to make the word *conjectured* were never solved.

Mom said, "Lizzie for Pete's sake! Will you stop reading us every grisly detail you come across?"

"Will I have to testify?" I asked Rob the Scarecrow, who was now practically living with us and was eating clam chowder with us that night. "Because I don't think I could stand to see him. Like if I had to go past him my whole body would shake so hard I wouldn't be able to speak."

Mom said, "Think how it will be for Julio. Having an uncle who is accused of murder, an uncle who kept you prisoner for a year. He has to tell the whole story all over again in court."

"You will have to testify because you are a witness, but I'm sure you won't have to go right past him," Rob said spearing the last piece of garlic bread out of the basket. "Anybody else want this? You'll have an advocate assigned to you by the court and whoever that is, he or she will keep you well away from the accused. Your advocate will not let them put you through the wringer. So let's cross that bridge when we come to it Lizzie."

I sort of knew *advocate*, from the Latin *ad*, for, and *vocare*, to speak. As for putting through a wringer, that's what women had to do in the old days before they had washing machines with spin cycles. Then I stopped and thought about all those women who have probably never even seen a washing machine and the millions of people who have to wash their clothes in the nearest river. I heard on the eight a.m. news on our local public radio station that Blanco was going to be arraigned this morning at ten. And then on the TV evening news there was a whole lot more. He was asked whether he *pled* guilty or not guilty to the list of charges that included holding his nephew in involuntary servitude, trafficking in endangered animals, which are the tamarins, and murdering the man named Carlos who had helped import them. He *pleaded* not guilty and was led away in shackles. (You have a choice of *pled* or *pleaded* and since I couldn't decide which, I used them both.) Even though I know he is a terrible man I hated to see those shackles. They made me think of slaves coming out of ships' holds and being taken to the auction block.

CHAPTER 22

$\mathcal{M}$om has been investigating the trip to the primate refuge in Georgia. In fact she and Jenna have been conspiring to arrange for a caravan of all of us to drive there. We would have to stay overnight in a motel because it is approximately 470 miles from Woodvale, Florida, to Old Harmony, Georgia, not too far from Savannah, and we would be on the road one night each way. Mom says some of the good motels have swimming pools, which is an attraction, but I'm already thinking that they may have cable TV and we might get to see some good movies.

Then I overheard her on the phone with a woman at the refuge in Old Harmony. She had a voice as loud as a sports announcer so it was hard not to overhear her. It went something like: "Good wukkers? They'ah ahnt eny good wukkers eny moah. They'ah just cum in an' one wik lateh they'ah wantin' they'ah paycheck an' they'ah outah heah."

Then I heard Mom describing Julio. "It's a long story but he ended up caring for the thirty-two tamarins you took in several weeks ago all on his own, and it is only thanks to him that they survived, so would you consider?"

And then that roaring voice saying, "Hail yes if he's

legal ah'd bless him raht inta tha' job a' keepin' the birthin' cages clean an' the new mothas looked afta. We'ah got ten new'uns—five sets'a twins. We'ah very strict heah, that means he'd hafta mejjuh up to ah stannarts."

So that was how I found out that the tamarins were reproducing.

Mom said, "I don't want to get his hopes up, but if Julio wants to travel to Georgia to see his monkeys . . ."

And then Teresa said, "Absolutely, we'll come too. I think it's a wonderful idea since Digger and I haven't had a real vacation for ages." Well, Rob was all in favor of Julio coming and I quote: "An excellent way to get this boy out of reach of the tentacles of *Los Pícaros*." And I think he wanted to be within reach of my mom. So that's how we got to be a caravan of three cars. Digger, Teresa, and Julio rode in one, Jenna and Josh in another, and my mom and me and Rob the Scarecrow, who had suddenly declared that he desperately needed to get out of Miami for a few days, in the third. All heading for the Old Harmony Refuge for New World Primates in Old Harmony, Georgia.

I guess we were quite a sight en route. I mean, at every stop out came two wheelchairs and in them the two crips and then the grown-ups and Julio, who got a lot of suspicious looks because he's Latino. It makes me pretty mad when I see people who are bigots. I never got to use the word *bigot* before. You might like to know there's a story about it that it goes back to Rollo, who was a Viking and became the first duke of Normandy. He supposedly refused to kiss the foot of the French King Charles III in the year 911 and said, "*by got.*" Probably he meant *by God I won't.*

Charles was also known as Charles the Simple but I couldn't find out why. It may just be a story to explain how bigot got to mean somebody who for no reason hates people who aren't just like him.

It was pretty comical sometimes, all of us unloading just to buy some sandwiches and juice or iced tea at the convenience stores attached to the gas stations, where "the facilities" were sometimes okay and sometimes disgusting. When they were disgusting I made a point of wheeling up to the cash register and telling the clerk loudly enough to be heard all through the store. I mean, I wasn't exactly the shot heard 'round the world but I think I made a tiny difference.

As for the motel going and coming, Josh and I did actually go swimming twice. This neat pool had steps with a big pole to hold onto and Josh and I could boost ourselves right into the shallow end. Julio did an awesome belly flop from the deep end to start us off. We stayed in taking turns playing Marco Polo till our fingers were prunes and we all were really bushed. In case you don't know the game, it's a kind of tag and the person who is "it" has to swim around with his eyes closed. The other person with his eyes open tries to stay away from him. The "it" player calls out "Marco" and the other player has to answer "Polo" and this goes on until the "it" player catches up with the other and tags him and then they change places.

And at night we got to see two terrible movies—sci-fi, which I hate, but Julio and Josh both love them, so I suffered along. I mean, I just can't get into these characters from different galaxies. I have enough trouble with our own mortals. "Mortals from Earth"—that's what they always call us and it gives me goosebumps every time.

Finally and none too soon, our destination! We didn't need the GPS to tell us we had arrived, with Old Harmony Bank on one corner and Old Harmony Feed and Grain Store cattycorner to it. The Old Harmony Café two doors down advertised sandwiches and cold drinks along with the coffee. Everything else in Old Harmony was the sanctuary. It had a special campus set aside for little New World monkeys, squirrel monkeys, spider monkeys, capuchins, and several kinds of tamarins. Most primate refuges deal with chimps, sometimes left over from the entertainment industry, and rhesus macaques, discarded from medical experiments. Old Harmony had some of these on a separate campus but the main focus was on the tamarins. Once we were all installed in a nearby motel which incidentally didn't have a pool, we went over to meet the director, Ms. Marybel Goodspeed, who turned out to be the woman with the loud voice.

Digger wore his chief of police uniform to make the visit look more official but as it turned out he didn't need to because Marybel Goodspeed was used to all kinds of official visits from governors to health officers to the FBI tracking down points of origin for stolen primates.

What I liked about Marybel was she never once asked about the wheelchairs. She talked to us like normals. She took one look at Julio who saved all those tamarins and hugged him! He just stood there wrapped in her arms wondering what had happened. Her Southern accent was harder than Spanish but we gradually got the hang of it.

And let's face it, think how we sound to her. Like creatures from a foreign country, I bet. We talk through our noses and people in New England put *r*'s on the ends of things like *parkar* and *drawr*. And what about *sawr*? I sawr a bird. That made me think about Henry and his *flors* and *strub-bries* and wanting *a'sister livin'* for his mother. I sort of wished he could have come along and seen Old Harmony.

Then we all got a tour of the campus where lots of the monkeys had been used in the Air Force space experiments and in medical research, which you don't want to know about, believe me. Some with only one hand, two blind chimps, some looking starved from having been used to test the toxic effects of certain medicines. Those crippled monkeys had been through a lot.

After that, she took us out to the New World's forest, that's what she called it, only it came out *fahest*, and at first I thought she was saying *farthest* but then I caught on. There were several rescued capuchins—some people call them organ-grinder monkeys—and squirrel monkeys she said had been captured in Colombia and put up for sale. The tamarins were living in a cluster of live oaks with lots of nests up high and plenty of bushes growing in what is known as the understory. It wasn't a rain forest but it looked very airy and nice and it was clean. There was a moat all around and a tall fence around the moat. Marybel said we couldn't go in because we would contaminate the monkeys and if Julio took the job he would have to be thoroughly disinfected before he could begin work. So he just stood outside their sanctuary and called to them in the same sort of chuckles and trills Trippy and I had heard that first day. He sounded just like them. You couldn't really be sure they were answering him or that they recognized his voice but the level of their chatter definitely went up. Marybel was impressed. She didn't say anything but there was an admiring look on her face so I thought that was a good sign.

There wasn't any paperwork involved because as Marybel said, "We'ah operatin on good faith." She and Julio shook hands on it. I thought he looked a little afraid she was going to hug him again. He was promised time off and airfare from Savannah to Miami when Jeb Blanco's case came to trial, which according to the Scarecrow might take a year, so we'll cross that bridge when we get to it. I think that's his favorite expression.

Another sweet thing is, the job came with an apartment on the grounds, which we did get to see. I thought it was pretty grim—one room with a bed, a table, and a lamp. And second room with the smallest fridge ever made plus a microwave and a hot plate, which is two burners to cook stuff on. Julio said, "This is a palace compared to the shack I was living in."

I had to agree. I can't really think of that shack without thinking of the trapdoor and the ladder and the whole . . . abduction.

Marybel said, "I think if things *wukk* out I might could locate a couch and a TV." She also said she would help him with his study plan for the GED exam. It turns out that The Hammer had already been helping him with his algebra, so he was rounding second base on the way to third. That was Rob's call.

Marybel thought the office computer could be freed for

Julio's use after five p.m. Mom said, "If you email me your English essays I will send them back with comments. Be sure you use the spelling and grammar app on the computer. It will help you to see where your mistakes are."

Still, it was hard saying goodbye to Julio. Everybody acted very cheerful but I felt sad. I've never been good at goodbyes so when he bent down to give me a half hug I had to pinch myself to keep from letting any tears leak out.

AFTERWORD

Well, Teresa has read my autobiography up to here and says she really likes it. I thought the ending might be too sad. But she pointed out that the book ends happily for the cubs and for Julio and that plenty of people's lives don't have happy endings, including rich movie stars.

And I said, "To say nothing of the millions of people who go to bed hungry every night."

"Also," Teresa said, "Digger might have another heart attack and I have to live with that fear every day."

That made me choke up.

I'm still really sad when I think about saying goodbye to Julio and I still feel scared when I think about that night in the root cellar. Sometimes I'm really angry about being probably stuck in a wheelchair for the rest of my life. But now that I'm practically an adolescent I can look back at everything that's happened with some perspective (from the Latin *per,* through and *specere,* to look). I've made some good new friends, not just the kind you email with. Josh and I still have to perfect our email shorthand since we aren't going to see each other for months at a time. Not just things like *yolo* which stands for you only live once and *rofl* for rolling on the floor laughing and *smh* for shaking my head. (It sort of makes me shake my head just writing these things down.) Tom and Aurelia will be getting married in ten days and I'll attend their wedding. I've got new honorary grandparents and a mom who's pretty special and it looks as though Rob the Scarecrow might be my father one day in the not-too-distant future. All in all, it's been quite a year. I'm definitely feeling ready for high school with my binocs and my Mac and my *American Heritage Dictionary*.

ABOUT THE AUTHOR

Honored as America's poet laureate from 1981 to 1982, MAXINE KUMIN has been the recipient of the Pulitzer Prize and many other awards. In addition to her seventeen poetry collections, novels, and essay collections for adults, she is the author of many children's books. Seven Stories Press is re-releasing four of Kumin's out-of-print children's books for kids ages five to eight, co-written with poet Anne Sexton: *Eggs of Things* and *More Eggs of Things* (illustrated by Leonard Shortall) and *Joey and the Birthday Present* and *The Wizard's Tears* (illustrated by Evaline Ness). She lived with her husband on a farm in the Mink Hills of Warner, New Hampshire, where they raised horses for forty years and enjoyed the companionship of several rescued dogs. She died in early 2014.

ABOUT THE ILLUSTRATOR

ELLIOTT GILBERT has illustrated and written numerous children's picture books including *Max Goes Hunting* and *My Cat Story*. Among the many books he has illustrated are *Mittens In May* by Maxine Kumin and the popular classic *The Best Loved Doll* by Rebecca Caudill. His paintings have been exhibited in many galleries and won numerous awards. Examples of his work can be seen on his website elliottgilbert.com. He lives with his wife in Hoboken, New Jersey.